红蓝如凌

RED BLUE RULING

张如凌 著
安德鲁 配画

Ruling Zhang

Paintings by Paul Andreu

上海人民出版社

图书在版编目(CIP)数据

红蓝如凌/张如凌著. —上海:上海人民出版社,
2016

ISBN 978-7-208-14130-8

Ⅰ.①红… Ⅱ.①张… Ⅲ.①诗集-中国-当代
Ⅳ.①I227

中国版本图书馆 CIP 数据核字(2016)第 246877 号

责任编辑 舒光浩 陈佳妮
装帧设计 包晨晖
设计制作 王蓬子 李莹君

红蓝如凌

张如凌 著

世纪出版集团

上海人民出版社出版

(200001 上海福建中路 193 号 www.ewen.co)

世纪出版集团发行中心发行 常熟市新骅印刷有限公司印刷

开本 635×965 1/16 印张 19.5 插页 2 字数 180,000

2016 年 10 月第 1 版 2016 年 10 月第 1 次印刷

ISBN 978-7-208-14130-8/I·1593

定价 68.00 元

献给关爱我的人

鸣谢

ACKNOWLEDGEMENTS

由衷感谢所有为此书的出版付出心血和智慧的前辈、朋友和家人：

Special thanks to my masters, friends, and family for their great contributions to the publication of this poetry book :

保罗·安德鲁 Paul Andreu	白桦 Bai Hua	骆寒超 Luo Hanchao	赵丽宏 Zhao Lihong
陈昕 Chen Xin	王为松 Wang Weisong	舒光浩 Shu Guanghao	陈佳妮 Chen Jiani
包晨晖 Bao Chenhui	张云兰 Zhang Yunlan	江慎 Robert Johnson	张英嫘 Zhang Yinglei
白潇客 Jacques Blein	司马浩 Robbie Smitheram	白雪涛 Alexandre Blein	

安德鲁作品 1号

梦中的汗血宝马

赵丽宏

我晾出满手宝石
如数家珍
一阵风
将它们吹上天
变成满天星斗闪烁

这是张如凌诗作《我绕过记忆》中的诗句。诗歌如宝石，从她手中晾出，其实是从她灵魂里涌出。它们飞上天穹，变成闪烁的星斗……读这样的诗，不仅感叹诗人的想象力，也感佩她的自信。她确实有这种自信的底气，我眼前的这本诗集《红蓝如凌》，是一个很有说服力的证明。我是断断续续读完这本诗集的，阅读的过程中，常常陷入遐想，她的诗作，不时引起我的共鸣，也引发我的思索。

毫无疑问，张如凌是一位才华横溢的女诗人，她既有东方襟怀，也有西方情韵。她在《致诗人》中宣告：『你既然是诗人／就不能只有一片天空／一块土地／你既然是叛逆的诗人／就应该去浪迹天涯／眺望另一片天空／游走另一块土地』。她生在中国江南，中华文化为她的诗歌创作夯下厚实的底蕴，她长期在欧洲游历，西方文化开拓了她的视野，两种文化，在她的诗中有美妙的碰撞，也有水乳交汇般的融合。《远古的呼唤》是一首描绘梦境的诗，构思奇特，意境幽邃，而蕴含期间的深情，让人回味不尽。诗人在法国诺曼底海边做着古老的中国梦，梦醒时分，历史和现实融为一体，时空失去了距离：

昨夜。梦里
我亲爱的马走了
那匹深褐色的汗血宝马
沿着诸暨浣溪河边
一个清凉寂静的中秋夜
圣洁的月光照引它
朝春秋国广漠的草原去了
是载着美女西施上的路

她是吴王夫差心爱的女人
同去找三千年前的家园
追逐梦。无韁疾驰
早该让它奔向远古的
属于它的岁月
如此洒脱。无牵挂

梦醒。泪如雨下
是马蹄声惊了我
窗外。白沙滩
诺曼底海边的马场
一对恋人欢笑着
骑着汗血宝马
驰骋远去……

她在诗中说梦，在梦中寻诗，对故乡的深情，对岁月的感叹，对爱情的向往，凝聚在一首短

短的诗中，寄付在那匹汗血宝马的蹄声中，飞过海滩，穿越时光，那种深长曲折的意蕴，让人读之心颤。

如凌的诗，有天马行空的自由遐想，她在《冥想》中「飞越天际/与永恒拔河」。她云游天下，笔锋一转，便飞越万水千山，然而不管身在何方，故乡和亲人，都是她诗中无法分离的主角。她在诗中写乡愁，写情爱，写杭州西湖烟雨，写上海复兴路上的梧桐树，写岁月的沧桑，写人生的悲欢离合，都饱含着真挚的情意。她的诗中没有空泛之词，她在自己熟悉的生活中寻获灵感，捕捉诗意，她诗中出现的意象，都蕴涵着引人思索的深意。诗集中那些抒发对父母的思念、感恩和爱的诗作，尤其感人。

如凌不是职业写作者，她有轰轰烈烈的成功事业，让人惊奇的是，她竟然有精力和时间写诗。然而从她的诗中感觉到的，绝非忙碌和浮躁，而是一种沉静，是对人性的思索，对生活的挚爱。

她在喧嚣的市声中「给灵感挪出空间/捡回一路丢失的诗句」，她把理想中的诗篇比作钟乳石和琥珀，必须在洞穴中养精蓄锐慢慢生长，在地下深埋千年而臻圆润完美。她拒绝平庸，在诗中展现着自己的个性，也表达着对生命的独特思考。如《沉香醉》这首诗，便体现了她的追求。在诗人笔下，沉香之馨香，竟源自「一场情感浩劫/遍体鳞伤/痛着/欲罢不能」。其中的傲骨美德，令人感伤，那是「残缺的审美，残忍的沉醉」。这样的意象和境界，是如凌独到的发现。

稍纵即逝的时光，是张如凌诗中经常出现的主题，或许可以说，这也是隐含在她诗作中的一个永恒主题。诗集中有一首诗题为《来不及》，是表现这个主题的奇妙之作，不同的读者，可以从中品悟出不同的情境。时光从每个人身边飞过，留下了什么？如凌将她与众不同的感受定格在她的诗句中：

梦中传来你熟悉的呼唤
焦虑的我只挪着碎步
来不及牵手已然转身告别

睡梦里你叩响了我的门
微笑间添了几道皱纹
来不及触摸你却离我远去

二〇一六年八月十四日于上海四步斋

诗歌是心灵的净土

骆寒超

我和女诗人张如凌结识纯属偶然。那是几年前，诗人白桦向我供职的《星河》诗刊荐诗，是一组如凌写的爱情诗。它们显得热烈、真诚、闪烁着单纯美的洁光，还可以见出作者的诗歌修养不浅，诗也就都发了。后来就收到了她寄赠的两本中英文对照的诗集《中国红》《法国蓝》，才知道她是旅法华裔，在美、法最高学府完成了现代诗歌的理论研究后，却在巴黎从事建筑美学的职业工作。在国外打拼三十多年，事业有成，还曾获法国政府授予『国家功勋骑士勋章』和『国家功勋军官勋章』，应该说这已是不平凡的人生经历，她尽可以享受异国情调的安逸生活了，可她不！因了职业的需要，更为了对故土的思念，她一年有好几次回上海，徘徊在复兴路上，吟哦在黄浦江边。那两本诗集就是她在东西方两种文化相交叠的背景下写成的。集子中两种乡恋，两类乡愁绞在一起的抒情，其动人之处可说为当代中国提供了一道别具格局、另样色彩的诗坛风景，使我不禁也为她抒情事业取得的成就而感动。前不久，如凌来杭州，我们在西子湖边见面，品茶谈诗之余，她拿出一叠诗作打印稿，说这是她准备出版的第三本诗集，让我看看，还说如果可以，为它写篇序。于是我也就成了这本题为《红蓝如凌》的诗集的第一个读者。读罢全稿，掩卷沉思，深感如凌这部新作颇有一些新的诗情内容，诗艺上也有相当的进展，所以也就决定来说上几句。

《红蓝如凌》单从题名上看似乎就已表明着如凌在这本新作中有一个抒情新意图，要把抒唱中国「红」的热烈鲜亮与抒唱法国「蓝」的冷艳清远融成一体，来对以全球为家的乡恋乡愁、以对现代生态的情爱和谐作热烈而清远、冷艳而鲜亮的综合抒情了。我这场「望文生义」的猜想看来没有错，因为诗集给我的最深刻印象就是如凌面对人类生态所作的情爱和谐倾诉，心怀全球视野所作的乡恋乡愁抒唱。值得指出：在这本诗集中隐藏着一个新颖的抒情逻辑：情爱必须通向和谐，和谐是情爱的升华；乡恋必然通向乡愁，乡愁是乡恋的升华。这个抒情逻辑的存在反映着女诗人挚爱人生的纯洁，这在《回归大地》《岁月已黄昏》《如果你允许》《春江花月夜》等作品中都相当动人地体现着。不妨来谈谈《回归大地》。这首诗是抒情主人公对所爱者所怀永恒之恋的倾诉，说：「爱人，浪迹天涯的旅途/你说过相约与我走完」，可是渐行渐远地已「到血染夕阳」时分，难道还能「来一段人生探戈」——让青春像圆舞曲那样循环地回来吗？当然已不可能了。

但『纵使留不住青春』，只要有『誓言』的永恒也就够了。这是对情爱欲求的升华——只求永远心心相印，共享灵性生命的和谐。但这还不够，诗篇进一步展开痴想，说要和『爱人』一起带着『我们的诗』飞向『天鹅座的行星』，将他们『亘古的传奇』在另一个天体中延续，而让肉身『赤裸着还给了清白的大地』，这可是『身本洁来还洁去』的事儿——一种对地球存在来说也是大和谐的肉性生命追求，给人以热烈而清远之感。类似的追求在《岁月已黄昏》中还显得更加感人。这些情爱诗在这本诗集中虽然占有相当一部分，好像在对生命的欲念寻求作抒唱，其实更显现为一种本体象征，象征着囊括人类本体灵肉大和谐的祈盼。这个抒情逻辑的存在更反映着女诗人依恋世界的深情。这在《秋天的梧桐》《暮秋的虚度》《超度今生》《夜游西湖》等作中也相当动人地体现着。在《超度今生》中，如凌说自己有『一种精神追逐』，像『孤寂中守候千帆过尽』一样。这追逐的对象所指者谁？原来是当年『在市井深巷望天空』所见到的那轮『故乡的月亮』，是经历了『八千里云雨』的奔波而让他乡成了自己新的家园后油然而生的那一缕对故土的乡恋。可是当她又经历『八千里云雨』的奔波回到故土，进入『老屋』，让乡恋如愿以偿后，浮上心头的却是『走出老屋只见虚无』——故土的家园毕竟成了虚无的存在，自己真实的家园其实已在遥远的塞纳河边，于是在『流年太轻。云飘无痕』的天地间『我』这名过客又『该辞行了』，——

回到新的家园去。可是在远方那『新筑的楼台亭阁』又怎能承载自己『今生的超度』呢？是的，对一个深情地依恋世界的女诗人来说，这广大的世界其实处处是故乡，能诱发她的乡恋，但故乡又总会变他乡，所以也就处处会有乡愁了。这些正是对世界怀有深情的这位全球为家者自我精神追逐中显示出来的一场冷艳而又鲜亮的表现。类似的表现在《秋天的梧桐》中显得更能促人深思。除以上一些诗例，这里我还想特别提一提令人读后久久难忘的一首诗：《远古的呼唤》：深夜，梦中，一匹汗血马在中国的苎萝山下浣纱溪边负上美女西施奔向三千年前的春秋国去了，去寻找失散的夫君吴王夫差，同他一起去找回失去的家园……但这时梦醒了。『泪如雨下』的『我』在马蹄声中却望见：

窗外。白沙滩
诺曼底海边的马场
一对恋人欢笑着
骑着汗血宝马
驰骋远去……

这是一场把情爱和谐与乡恋乡愁结合起来的奇思，这是一场让历史从悲慨转向和谐、让人类从乡愁转向乡恋融汇在一起的妙想，这更是一场地球村终于走向和谐的生态大合唱。

于是我们听到这位浪游世界、情寄天涯的华裔女诗人真挚的心声了：热烈而清远，冷艳而鲜亮。

而《远古的呼唤》更令我感兴趣的是它标志着如下这点：如凌已从任随心潮起伏而作纯内在倾诉的那种诗歌写作习惯中挣脱出来，寻求一条立足实际生活触发而作由外而内抒情的路子。这对她来说可是全新的。这首诗能在时间与空间、历史与现实、东方与西方相交叠中展开艺术构思，且显得神幻、真切、融合，是同她曾漫游于故国越地一隅的浣纱溪和法兰西边陲的诺曼底所见所感而引发联想有决定性关系的。在诗歌创作中纯内在抒情只能是一种做法，对内感觉敏锐的诗人来说较合适，但这种写法容易把诗歌引向晦涩或空泛。追求生活实感，提倡由外而内再由内而外，在我看来是必要的。所以，如凌这条抒情新路值得赞赏。《大漠深处》《暮秋的虚度》《天边来客》都是这方面有代表性的追求。《大漠深处》一开头就说在沙漠里行走，放眼天地，就感到『人是渺小的／生命是短促的』。这是来自外在世界的实感。而接着的两节则根据实感而展开了超常的联想，第二节说沙漠是『洪荒之前／死去的世界』；第三节说大漠深处的『光阴』，都是『无忧无虑地／在此飘悠着』。这种联想让人感到主体已进入绝时空深处，有点匪夷所思了。以此构筑成的意象，则促人在想入非非中品尝到一点神异、高远、旷古的美感。如果主体没有投入客观世界，触发起生活实感，哪能把握到这些奇思妙想。《暮秋的虚度》在我的印象中是一首写得完整、有机而具有融和之美的好诗，它以意境的浓郁而又清旷显出了较高的艺术层次，而这又完全要归功于它出于生活实感。诗所写的是在繁忙的工作之余，如凌在暮秋时分难得地度过一个平淡的下午。全作把她对休憩家中的想象联缀成篇，所以是一篇类似漫兴之作。如写她欣赏飘满黄叶的花园时的情景：『我倦怠地倚窗／想抓几片正飘落的枫叶／飘得如此轻盈／我用双手都接不住』。又如遥望巴黎晴空：『望着与世无争的白云／无拘无束地飘逸着／在我眼前停留后又飘走／这景象有几分感伤／又有几分温柔／一种虚无缥缈的感觉／笼罩着我』。这种种表现真正是一场信手拈来、脱口而吟、意趣无穷的事儿，却也全凭依她投入外象抓住实感，于漫不经心中构筑成一个意象组合体，从中感兴出一片意境才得以达到的。意境不是实实在在可以把握住的实体，而是接受者通过诗人营构的意象及其组合体所触发出来的感觉刺激在心灵中获得审美感应的产物，所以意境实是存在于接受者心中的一种飘忽的感性体验。从这个意义上说，意境的生成更多地依赖于外物及对外物的实感。如凌这一场从纯内在倾诉转为由外而内的抒情，也就决定了她这本新作就比《中国红》《法国蓝》中的诗要有意境得多。在这首《暮秋的虚度》中有两处说『好久没这感觉了』，这感觉其实就是她所向往的清静平淡生活，就凭此而她在诗中营构了一串串意象及其组合体，并把它们提供给了读者的我们，才使我们在对这些意象及其组合体作具体而真切的体验中品尝到了如此浓郁而又飘忽的意境美。

还值得提一提的是，如凌这场从纯内在倾诉转向投入外在实际生活而作由外而内的抒情，还反映出了她对客观世界作密切关注的兴趣。具体点说，她已能在一定的程度上把灵感赋予时弊针砭上，写下了《谎言》《天边来客》等匡正世风之作，这是值得肯定的。但我认为走向外在世界对如凌来说还有一点重要意义是：使她在一定程度上对中国传统诗学作了超越，接纳了属于世界潮流的现代诗写作经验。现代诗的时尚化我并不赞成，但现代诗中有一些诗情境界与传达技巧确有可取之点，是不能不承认的。如凌不是个时尚的弄潮儿，但对一些确有可取的东西她倒也来者不拒。对知性、对拟想的奇特、对意象变形象征、对荒诞表现、对语言的张力追求等，这些她都尝试着使用起来了，并在这本新作的某些文本建构中，留下深深浅浅的脚印。有人说她的诗近来有些变了。这个感觉是确实的，我也有。变就变在某些现代诗风的新格局在她的近作中已有出现。《我绕过记忆》《梦幻的真实》《心语》等作品，就是体现现代诗风格技巧相当成功之作。《我绕过记忆》是一首献身于世界纯洁化这场宏伟事业的梦幻诗。全作以对海天间壮阔的宇宙境界作出雄浑的抒情来象征『我』处于人间沧桑中的一份『守望海天之间的变化』的精神责任感。『我』

既想要在蓝色的海洋深处探求「宝石」，让「一阵风／将它们吹上天／变成漫天星斗闪烁」，又要想扫荡尽「雪崩后」浮出海面的「冰川纪的遗物」——「泛滥成无法治理的海藻」。诗篇在最后一节中提纯出一点知性意悟：

万年都只在瞬间
我守住的最后防线
不过是海天一线
刹那的永恒

是的，刹那寓永恒，永恒在刹那！这样的抒情让人感受到一种俊逸的知悟，知悟的壮阔，壮阔的精神献身图景。这样的现代诗知悟境界追求，格调是高的，可以见出如凌不是个雕虫小技的耽爱者、卖弄者。

如凌这批近作在语言上，颇有些警句、隽语，留给人很丰富的遐想，如「黄昏蓄满成熟的眷恋」（《晨与暮》），「追不上的光年是我的归宿」（《千古绝唱》），「当最后一缕余晖／舔去我灵魂流下的泪珠』(《孤独的灵魂》)、『月色泻下完美的寂寞』(《夜游西湖》),等等。在谋篇上,也有很讲究构思的,如《岁月已黄昏》《远古的呼唤》等;在意象营构及其组合上,有的极精致巧妙,如《今夜难眠》中有:『消瘦的月亮疼了忧郁的心』,这月的『消瘦』感和『疼』了心的拟喻化意象就极佳。从总体看来,这些近作是如凌认真琢磨出来的。诚如她在《心语》一诗中说的:『颠覆文字挥霍细节/卧薪尝胆打磨洁净的灵魂/这是我一生心语的积淀』!说得多神圣!这也就决定了这本诗集已上了艺术新层次。

也许有人会这样问:张如凌为什么这样痴情于诗?那就听听她在《梦幻的真实》中的一句话:『诗歌是我心灵的净土』!

二〇一六年八月十二日写于

浙江大学求是村

目次

辑一

孤独的灵魂

辑二

迟到的绽放

目次

辑三

沉香醉

目次

辑四 异乡人在天涯

目次

辑五

动心的那一刻

辑一

孤独的灵魂

红蓝如凌

习惯了在蓝天白云中
自由地凌空翱翔
任由结局如何
早已确定了高度

从蓝天上俯瞰
山不再高
海不再宽
我拎着阳光

让遐想随云飞翔

穿云破雾
感悟天幕无垠
斑斓的彩虹
留一抹红蓝辉映
思绪久久驰骋其中……

剪下最后一缕夕阳
夹入诗页中回忆
伴随灵魂飘落
红蓝如凌
留一片冰心
或是久远
或是淡忘

心语

致诗人赵丽宏

钟乳石躲在潮湿的洞穴
养精蓄锐百年生一厘
才得以让世人观赏感叹

琥珀深埋地下千万年
色泽方显圆润完美
才能换得收藏者青睐

在天地间寻觅冰川风化

唯有沧海桑田起变迁
才可造就这亘古的诺言

诗人笔下遗留的诗篇
千年沉浮后仍流传
才算嵌入岁月的经典

颠覆文字挥霍细节
卧薪尝胆打磨洁净的灵魂
这是我一生心语的积淀

你若会听
人间永是四月天

致诗人

诗人
不要再沉沦
听我说
你不该被遗忘

你既然是诗人
就不能只有
一片天空
一块土地

你既然是叛逆的诗人
就应该去浪迹天涯
眺望另一片天空
游走另一块土地

你既然是浪漫的诗人
就快舒展你的双臂
拥抱这满天星光
感受苍穹的浩瀚

你既然是感伤的诗人
就不应再搜集悲哀
不要沉迷于揭伤

痛楚之后更凝练

你既然是敏锐的诗人
就该懂我爱的尊严
黎明前我会隐去
将幻想留给黑夜

你既然已是诗人
就赶快去寻回
丢失的年华
消失的新月

诗人

不要再失落
听我的
你不会被磨灭

如果你允许

诗人
看见你那双深邃的眼睛
忘却了个人的凄凉
我愿为你分担忧愁
只因我懂你
如果你允许

诗人
看见你那双忧郁的眼睛
不忍心再让你牵挂

我愿用此生阅读你
只因我敬你
如果你允许

诗人
看见你那双炽热的眼睛
抛弃了过往的寻觅
余生就让我来陪伴
只因我爱你
如果你允许

诗人
看见你那双睿智的眼睛

瞬间穿透我的心灵
老时请让我来深爱
只因我疼你
如果你允许

诗魂

致前辈骆寒超

你为蓝天托起白云
我看到遥远的距离
试图穿越想象的空间

你给黑夜点燃星斗
无尽长夜有了期盼
梦想在万水千山中绵延

你赐我一张白纸

留下数不清的悬念
写诗的欲望在旷野中驰骋

诗句之间
你替我留白
这是灵魂间的呼唤

每写一首诗
都有你的批注
诗骨架起了灵肉的身段

夜深沉
你转身离开

留下诗韵在群星间

黎明前
我捡起你的妙语精华
抑扬顿挫中执意雕琢绝美诗篇

春华秋实一挥间
诗里行间跳跃的音韵光影
是过往沧桑灵魂留下的咏叹调

孤独的灵魂

当最后一缕余辉
舔去我灵魂流下的泪珠
古老昏暗的路灯
瞬间准确地摆起阵势
赤裸着向我挑逗
泛黄而下坠的乳房
预告它们的衰老
而且已经有些年头

前人设计的爱情间距
重复地将我的影子
亲吻后重新抛弃
我找不到归宿

爱情翻开太久
开始陈旧了
该用些闪光的诗句
嵌入失语的天空
展现碰撞与交替的痕迹

爱情挥霍太多
开始斑驳了

穿过情感的荒凉
大雁在沉寂的夜空
一声挥泪呼唤
击中了我孤独的灵魂

我给爱情重新命名
再将小夜曲的慢板拉长
路灯下唱得几近完美
有了心灵的感应
多几分岁月的蹉跎
冥冥中听到你的誓言
纵然天各一方
也可以承载刻骨铭心

春江花月夜

观同名昆剧有感

我们一出场
就是一个辉煌惊艳
一生琢磨如何入戏
将人物塑造得栩栩如生
戏如人生　人生如戏
我们做到了

记得吗　那可是我们的年华
或是人物饱满　出语惊人

使人震撼厚重

怎会忘　那都是我们的真情
或是轻盈飘过　活色生香
使人伤感疼惜

我们一亮相
就是台下掌声经久不息
我们有太多追捧者
只要我们上戏
就有人投情落泪至终
千回百转
用心演绎真实人生

我们曾经是真正的角儿

人间没有不散的戏
再担纲最后一次角儿
相约在今晚
《春江花月夜》
如若爱有来生
我们还携手追寻

这是我们寻觅的最高境界
这是我们此生最美的姿态

大戏终于圆满落幕

在这人生舞台
我们手挽手
庄严地谢了幕
不再羁绊今生束缚
天若有情天不老
宿命的相逢还会有来世

又见父亲

一个不安宁的盛夏
塞纳河水漫堤岸
独自伤悲怀旧
夜半又见到了父亲……

梦见三十五年前：
与家人拥抱挥别
在去旧金山的飞机上
翻开那红色缎面小本：

『小女谨记』
父亲连夜为我写家训
一本留给女儿的诗集
是他赠我的唯一礼物
我含着泪一遍遍读着
父亲的人格气节
在字里行间流露

梦里，他的诗句在耳旁萦绕
我动笔写下：『我的父亲——
上海基督教家庭的进步青年
为拯救民族去延安追寻理想
这是一份信念，一个坚守

他坎坷的一生足以见证。』

接着，又梦见了那一场景
斯坦福大学。姐姐来看我
告诉我父亲走了。没能等我
我不相信这是真的。真的不信
我大声哭着：『爸爸没等我？
这不可能！说好了等我的。』
没想到与他的一别竟是永别

早知道这样我该留在他身边
再多抚摸一次他沧桑的皱纹
多看一眼他对我含笑的嘴角

不，这不是真的，是在梦里

我依稀仍在梦里游走：
当年的父亲清俊洒脱
就在延安宝塔山下
明媚的阳光普照
笑得那么灿烂
童年的我过早出现在岁月中
父亲骑着白马一路风尘
向我飞驰而来
我还没来得及叫他一声『爸』
他已转身赶去鲁迅艺术学院
他正忙着上课作曲

我在窑洞外听着
等着他带我回家
没留神他又去了黄河边
指挥起大家唱『交公粮』
好伯伯作词父亲来谱曲
这首歌曾唱得家喻户晓
我怎能不会

接着，又唱起了『豌豆角』：
『豌豆角角开紫花，
宝贝心肝快长大。
快长大呀快长大，
跟着八路打天下。』

这脍炙人口的摇篮曲
是爸爸写的，自幼就会了
我便跟着大家一起唱
比谁都唱得响、唱得好
还没听他夸奖我
他又骑着马赶去晋绥老区了……

再后来，我却梦见他：
戴着高帽子挂着牌子
被红卫兵绑着游街示众
我在人群里喊着叫着：
『他不是走资派，他是我爸。
他不是国民党特务，

他是抗日救国青年，他是好人！』
还没等我叫第二遍
就有人打我，将我抓走了
我大声哭喊着：
『爸爸，快来救我！』

我被自己的哭声惊醒了
醒来已是三十五年后的今天

梦醒后我好生惊讶
今天是他百年寿诞

父亲一生戎马倥偬

千秋功名何需评说
山川有证日月可鉴
父亲，您安息吧！
您的故事我会慢慢来说……

瞻仰钢琴诗人肖邦

与儿、侄一同圆梦

终于踏上肖邦的故土
半个多世纪的等待
肖邦的灵魂还在
华沙明媚的阳光下畅游
潺潺流水 鸟语花香
是肖邦在倾述故乡情
弹指一挥间的乡愁
却永远也挥不去

虽然他安息在一个半世纪前
我却听到了华尔兹的优雅旋律
玛祖卡轻快跳跃的节奏
波洛涅兹舞的欢快和深沉
更听到小夜曲梦幻般和谐动人

当之无愧的钢琴天才
他手里流出的每一首乐曲
都是诗情画意声貌并存的杰作
心灵在坦诉衷肠
用深深的情怀和泪水
细腻地诉说着乡愁
面对山河破碎

有家不能归
一颗年轻热诚的心
彻底崩溃了

巴黎收留了他
乔治·桑的爱
治愈了他的伤痛与悲哀
创作的激情重新点燃
这是他生命中最美丽的年华
内心的乡愁
民族与个人的悲凉
不懈地思索寻求
最终演绎了

情到深处的最高境界

故园和异乡的撞击对比
诗歌与音乐间相融的绝配
古典和现代的和谐流畅
技巧与情感完美结合
完全做到了极致
他无愧于美名
前无古人后无来者

是的，只有他
客死异乡后
整个巴黎给了他最高的圣典

他的身躯永远安息在拉兹公墓
全世界爱戴他的人都来瞻仰
墓碑前，至今还有未启封的情书
他那颗永远活着的心却送回了故乡
他是这个世界的唯一
唯一美的神话——钢琴诗人

在华沙肖邦博物馆
我们用他作的《葬礼进行曲》
为他送行超度
三十九岁，多么美好的青春
一颗璀璨的明星
在世人心里永不泯灭

辑二

迟到的绽放

春天的诱惑

春天来了
过早地来了
来得这么突然
天地还未备好新装
她却裸露着告诏宇宙

春天热情地向我们致敬
我看见了缤纷绚烂的色彩
我听见了百花盛开的声息

我闻到了土地润物的芳香
这是我期盼许久的奢华

春意盎然中
大地散发着欲望
如此骚动不安
欲罢却又不止
春天荡漾着幻想

春天的诱惑
来得干练猛烈
势不可挡
冬眠冻僵的爱情

彻底苏醒了

天鹅美丽婀娜
正努力孕育着生命
春日之于它们的
就是赤胆忠心
洁身自好

人之初的爱恋
始于春色的诱惑
相爱的人们在一起

就奢望永久虚度时光
既然爱着就享受春天的特权

云烟

山之巅
白云缭绕
走近飘逸如烟
抓住是两手湿润的空
滴落成雨
留下是幻想
轻柔的新梦随之飞翔
就让它在天边飘着 漾着
这样真好

烟雨西湖

致白林女士★

西子湖睡着
在江南的土地上
静静地躺卧了千年
流淌出世代诗人的韵味

西子湖美在它包容
可以将山峦拥进怀抱
却并不想占有

与雷峰塔默契成一种精神
在水天之间
互相承受理解
多情纤细的垂柳
压下了姿态来弥补轻浮

西子湖美在它宁静
一湖春水细腻成情丝
繁衍出亭亭玉立的荷花
仲夏夜飘来暗香醉人
娇艳了满湖倒影
绚丽多彩的云朵
为它摆出可比的对仗

朴实的湖水只透着仰望的淡然

西子湖美在它含蓄
收拢天地的精华而不炫耀
领略过千年的风花雪月
翻卷过百年的爱恨涟漪
最终不忘柳浪闻莺处
留一湖秋波给人间
这无关红尘风月
只因有爱

这是我眷恋已久的西子湖
烟雨朦胧时我如期而至

追随唐宋诗人的风骚
与诗友寻梦湿足
兑现情感的深度落魄
给灵感挪出空间
捡回一路丢失的诗句
这夜我与西湖同梦

*白林：
法国原驻华大使

夜游西湖

梦里我用千万种思念
捧着一颗破碎的心
在宁静的月光下
与你独自相遇
在中秋西湖

追寻你的踪迹
在你离开的地方
我用尽一生去铺垫
迎接你归来的那一刻

是苍穹下最庄严的重逢

浪游天涯只为久远的乡情
失落的岁月沉淀出圆满
沧桑中淡化所有细节
繁华荣耀早已褪落
用诚心开垦荒原

拾起你闪亮的诗
将思念隐藏进季节
月色泻下完美的寂寞
我把悲伤的心挂在天空
湖水倒印出一双裸体剪影

西湖风雨

仲夏的深夜
游人散尽
西湖宁静下来

雨不停地下
风不停地吹
西湖泛起涟漪
烟雨濛濛

我无家可归
独自一人
在苏堤上流连
将孤独的心
许诺给风雨西湖

雨没有家
风没有家
我也没有家
今夜我们心无羁绊
暗送温馨满西湖
这感觉唯独我们知道

潇潇，雨为我下
悠悠，风为我吹
今夜的我不再孤独

晨与暮

灿烂的晨曦
从黎明中苏醒
洋溢着清新的喜悦
散发生命的诱惑

夸下海口许诺
要征服万物生灵
定将光明留在天空
阳光璀璨永不落

骄阳正如日中天
光芒万丈普照大地
最终未抵御夕阳坠落
留一抹血红的意境

晨辉与夕照各自精彩
朝起暮落相隔一方
晚霞每秒的优雅变化
展显出消褪的深沉气度

黄昏蓄满成熟的眷恋
瞬间折射出隽永的精神

纵然只是宇宙的过客
天地间依然有梦憧憬无限

余晖

深秋 寒露降
夕阳开始悲壮起来
它正提着往日的辉煌
在寻找过冬的欲望
切不要去惊扰
更无需作别
天之外
你总能看到
它起落不息的繁忙

暮秋的虚度

晴朗的暮秋下午
阳光从斑斓的树叶中
泼泻般闯入窗内
如此骄奢淫逸
骚乱了我的思绪
无心再专注案边文书
巴黎的天随着云游
难得的周日放晴

姑且放纵自己
好久没这感觉了

昨晚雨下了一夜
窗外的花园里
早已落满了黄叶
我倦怠地倚窗
想抓几片正飘落的枫叶
飘得如此轻盈
我用双手都接不住

望着与世无争的白云
无拘无束地飘逸着

在我眼前停留后又飘走
这景象有几分感伤
又有几分温柔
一种虚无缥缈的感觉
笼罩着我

沏上一壶下午茶
独自慢慢品味
难得的清静
难得如此平淡

在这样平淡的秋日下午
想着一些平淡的过往

免不了回味踌躇
就这样平淡地虚度
好久没这感觉了

秋天的梧桐

西风将最后的梧桐吹落
深夜踩着满地的黄叶
独自走在复兴路上
此时夜很静
心也很静

所有繁华都黯淡了
倾听落叶的声音

呼吸它残存的余香
静静地感受秋天的空灵
和流年的痕迹

至今我已经不记得
多少次在复兴路漫步
又多少次踩着梧桐流连
我一直喜欢这种感觉
无论在故园或他乡

梧桐树带走了乡愁
因了幼时的梦想
竟在它的国度

抖落了满地痴情
终不知落叶归何处

迟到的绽放

漫长的寒冬
伤了我的心后
终究还是弃我而去了
春意暧昧不明
吝啬得姗姗来迟
玉兰花再高洁
也没抵抗住
早春冰雹的来袭
花姿疲惫
早衰了

春光明媚后
粉色绚烂的樱花
就此怒放了
开得情深意切
真实难舍
可被春风得意时一吹
就剩下轻薄命相了
花瓣缤纷落地
惹得我好生怜香惜玉
含泪葬花
且为痛彼此命运
郁金香娇艳受宠

花期太短，经不起炫耀
欲多观赏几番
竟无可奈何谢我而去
好一个悲命结局
只感叹空枝无所依

满园姹紫嫣红时
春雨却日夜交替地下着
泼洒了时日
尽兴后收敛了
无辜冲去几分春花姿色

卑微的紫丁香

总算奈住了寂寞
此时择机寻春
释放它弱小的承受
肆无忌弹地尽情开放
虽不与万花争艳
这实不起眼的花蕾
为求得我的关注怜爱
竟然纵情绽放一生
香飘满园沁人
终赢了我的芳心

待到丁香烂漫时
春天的童话便开始了

此刻我正柔情蜜意
等待你迟迟不到的归期

辑三

沉香醉

沉香醉

一场情感浩劫
遍体鳞伤
痛着
欲罢不能

点上陈旧的沉香残片
燃起袅袅青丝烟香
欲仙欲醉
驱了心中几多愁痛

沉醉于沉香的馨香
感伤其傲骨美德
唯真菌寄生
方能沉下香脂留世间

沉香沉
风烛残年
堪谓难能可贵
稀世尽在一木难求
安神定痛熏香

沉香沉

千年陈腐
形似枯竭的山石
亦作珍宝收藏
从古至今

如此残缺的审美
多么残忍的沉醉啊

大漠深处

在沙漠里行走
放眼望天地
人是渺小的
生命是短暂的

沙漠躺在亘古的宁静中
沉睡了亿万年
是洪荒之前
死去的世界

我们所追问所追寻的
为此而忽略的光阴
都无忧无虑地
在此飘悠着

我尽情感受在沙漠中
不倦地为人类写史诗
写我们无数世纪爱的故事
写完一页
悄悄藏起来
再写下一页
无休无止

我将写下的史诗
深埋进杳无人烟的大漠
千万年后
那些感人的章节
幻影般浮出
惊天地泣鬼神
风化成远古的遗址
等待后人来演绎
这一个个动人的传说

我绕过记忆

天马掠过的夜晚
我绕过记忆
守望天空

在蓝色海洋之上
有一扇眷顾我的大门
引我通往神秘花园
我晾出满手宝石
如数家珍
一阵风

将它们吹上天
变成满天星斗闪烁

海天之间
是你我的距离
近在咫尺之间
触手可及
远得天梯难抵
遥不可及

冰川纪的遗物
雪崩后开始浮出
竟在海上漂游繁殖

泛滥成无法治理的海藻
对大海来一次劫持
禁止它风情万种
断流涸泽
绝其念想
海洋才能干净

我绕过亿万年的记忆
仅守望海天之间的变化

万年都只在瞬间
我守住的最后防线
不过是海天一线
刹那的永恒

谎言

整个炎热的夏天
谎言喋喋不休
栽赃于挺直的橡树林
虚构成一个个破碎的细节
植入青春期的花序
未老先衰地迅速坠落

夏季的湖面
落叶惊慌失措
蓄满了凋零时的无奈

罂粟花一如泛紫的唇印
贴向失去记忆的湖水
沉沦前将灵魂作了升华

仅只在一夜间
封存的贞洁被盗
乱季中一度失态的人
掌控了局势
为了些蝇头小利
我莫须有成了故事的载体
余晖下试图打捞几许尊严
唯利是图的小鱼落网

且放它们生路
鱼儿感念我的慈悲
七秒钟的记忆
难能可贵

梦幻的真实

在梦幻的湖面上徜徉
努力寻找过往记忆
梦里的乡音
惊了我的乡愁
扰了我未醒的梦

沉浸在创作的灵感中
这是我安静的样子
诗歌是我心灵的净土

有人篡改了历史
就在烈日当空之下
偷梁换柱
只是一念之差
沿着前辈留下的废墟
寻找饶舌的瓦砾
虽挪动了碎片
却伤了自己的肝胆
当下急于拯救的是灵魂
灵魂脏了情感的天平作何评估

我的心思你不懂
前世今生只因有爱

我的乡愁你不懂
孤独中存放着无尽的企盼
灵魂的财富你不懂
宇宙间我收藏了
带不走的记忆

洪水灾难性地泛滥
淹没了的诗集
从此被人遗忘了
湖边一垂钓者
将它们钓起
在鱼竿上晾干
又翻开一页页赏读

他发现了隔世的星辰
金子般闪烁
消息不胫而走
世人们争先恐后
追逐起地球之外的
金星凌日之妙境

山雨欲来

肮脏的灵魂
在自由的国度
领取了合法通行证
狭窄的甬道
拥挤不堪
为争夺各自利益
互相伤害
我无法苟合求存
给他们让道

扭曲的人性
囤积了贪婪和仇恨
荒诞地暴露无遗
却大言不惭
要寻回自己的尊严
重返久远的殷实纯朴
锦缎包裹的方寸丢了视野
追逐奢华的流年失了法度
璀璨一时天地重新混沌
谬误充斥天空
我茫然惊骇不解

是时代堕落或道德疲劳
我预感山雨欲来
暴风雨将洗礼人类的良知

天边来客

地中海碗大的小岛
蓝天下的白沙滩
嬉海裸浴者的天堂
法兰西仅存的一片静土
至少尚未被污染
一抹阳光
投情于海洋
崇尚自然的裸浴男女
交替比美
轮回献爱

乍然间飞来五只海豚*
宁静中声音震耳
方寸下风沙飞扬
整个小岛都颤抖了
巨大的豪华型
来势凶猛
我认知它的产地
来自本土马赛

小岛上来了一群生人
为了朝圣大海
赶在同胞来袭之前

捷足先登风水宝地
清一色显露出土豪金气势
岛上的金发碧眼震惊了
哪路神仙下凡
要来此安寨扎营

坐拥岛上最昂贵别墅
旨在翻云覆雨间
饮食非公害
空气无雾霾
自由美丽的小岛
最佳逍遥圣地
不用忧虑

也不再纠结

我与他们说同种语言

新移民启程了

我无言自语

*海豚：

直升机的型号，产自法国马赛

猎人与梅花鹿

广袤的山林中
住着一位神枪手
热爱自然的异乡人

林中狩猎。湖中捕鱼
榛栗为食。花果作蔬
善良多情的猎手
呵护着珍稀野生动物
驯养其逃生技能

从黎明破晓至晚霞褪尽
那可爱美丽的梅花鹿
更是他忠诚相随的挚爱
真爱在他们之间传递

寒冬来临之前
小花鹿觅食敏捷
猎手亦需启程回故乡
彼此难舍难分

最后一次狩猎射击
晨曦刚染上霜降的山野
猎手正瞄准一只大野兔

扣下扳机的刹那
他心爱的梅花鹿冲上枪口
竟被一枪命中
倒在草丛中抽搐
这不是他的初衷啊

痛悔的猎手紧抱着它说：
『对不起，我亲爱的小鹿子！
告诉我，你为什么跑向我的枪口？』
美丽单纯的小鹿儿流着眼泪：
『因为爱！你明白吗？
难道不是吗？
我早该是你瞄准的猎物。

因为你爱上了我，
我才活得如此欢畅自由！』
『你的归期是我们诀别之日。
下一个猎手在冬雪飘落前，
定会毫不留情地射杀我。
今天我愿献上生命，
只因爱你太深。
能命丧你的枪下，
是我之幸，亦如我愿！』
『我崇拜的好猎手啊，
在我生命的终点，

请你答应我的愿望：
将我安葬在你的家园，
伴你度过余生。
我勇敢的猎手，
不要拒绝我卑微的请求吧……』

伤悲痛哭的猎手应诺了
梅花鹿在他怀中离去……

16.07.

辑四

异乡人在天涯

远古的呼唤

昨夜。梦里
我亲爱的马走了
那匹深褐色的汗血宝马
沿着诸暨浣溪河边
一个清凉寂静的中秋夜
圣洁的月光照引它
朝春秋国广漠的草原去了
是载着美女西施上的路
她是吴王夫差心爱的女人

同去找三千年前的家园
追逐梦。无缰疾驰
早该让它奔向远古的
属于它的岁月
如此洒脱。无牵挂

梦醒。泪如雨下
是马蹄声惊了我
窗外。白沙滩
诺曼底海边的马场
一对恋人欢笑着
骑着汗血宝马
驰骋远去……

望乡

观电影《望乡》有感

梦里忆到了
我去的山打根
一个美丽的小岛

我曾经走访了山打根
战时日本人望乡的岛屿
那是一段不为人知的历史
终身流落在此回不去的歌妓
在天一方隔海望故乡亲人

为生存栖小岛莺歌燕舞
山打根美得使人悲伤

山打根依然美得凄凉
它使我想起望乡人
在岛上留的墓碑

来不及

给你的诗在梦里闪烁
随风吹得一路洒落
来不及捡拾便被人掠夺

梦中传来你熟悉的呼唤
焦虑的我只挪着碎步
来不及牵手已然转身告别
睡梦里你叩响了我的门

微笑间添了几道皱纹
来不及触摸你却离我远去

梦醒后我已老态龙钟
笔锋苍劲感觉老到
来不及写世态就已陈旧

心灵深处的一道伤痕
前世今生隐藏不露
来不及悲叹流年已消逝

超度今生

崇高不在天地间繁衍
在人的灵魂中游走
一种精神追逐
孤寂中守候千帆过尽

真爱不寻风花雪月
也不与境界同梦
恰似行云流水
尘埃翻滚卷不起惊雷

生死度外的人
可被仰慕亦视卑微
天空不问人间事
人与云追赶
百转千回无尽头

市井深巷望天空
故乡的月亮可拽在手心
八千里云雨写进诗句
走出老屋只见虚无

流年太轻。云飘无痕

世道留不下感伤和脆弱
该辞行了
新筑的楼台亭阁
承载不了今生的超度

异乡人在天涯

异乡人的灵魂太重
你的双臂抱不动
异乡人的感伤太深
你的双眼看不透
异乡人的失望太多
你的抚慰已太迟

异乡人的行囊很轻
习惯独自走天涯

来时无忌去也无悔
天涯何处觅知音
说好了的承诺
忍痛抛向咫尺天堂

耽搁了些许光阴
异乡人上路了
消失在天涯

千古绝唱

冬至。罕见大雪
浦江两岸银装素裹
独自赏雪。好生感怀
五十年奇景
你我相遇的年份
心存念想，执意眺望远方
鹿瓦河谷。大雪纷飞
香堡宫殿尽显非凡霸气

五百年前
弗兰茨瓦献予挚爱
为红颜险失半壁江山
骑士国王凯旋归来冠英名

冰消雪融报以春花
浮光掠影挪不动英雄
城垣深深隔硝烟
有悦己者相伴
何曾寂寞
森林尽处骑马狩猎
田园山水中吟诗问梦
国王建筑师留一路辉煌

达芬奇神韵迄今绕梁
千秋功罪谁主沉浮

日月不同辉
花飘河谷几多世
你我前世香堡有约
也去狩猎骑马。也吟诗句
江山美如画
忘却天上人间
灵魂不死。生命轮回
我们信天堂誓言
开春。已是来世

浦江鹿瓦，两岸再牵手
生死如归
清明。香花香火来世也清淡
尘埃轻薄。我的诗也轻薄
烧去千古遗恨。作绝唱
追不上的光年是我的归宿
这样你我终究在天堂扯平了
你亦作何答？

母亲的遗孤

母亲，你是我浪迹天涯的思念
我是你日夜守望的牵挂
你将慈悲抱在怀里
我将乡愁捧在手心

自你走后
故乡不再收留我这遗孤
你去了蓝天之上
我的意念便飞去云霄

盼不到了，你我的人间重逢
母亲，女儿未尽之意
来日相见再回报
人间与天堂
仅在虚实一念间

母亲睡去了

母亲累了，
沉沉地睡着了。

那晚她在我怀里，
像一个无助的孩子，
用虚弱的眼神望着我。
试着蠕动嘴唇，
可一个字也说不出。
我紧紧地搂着她：

『宝贝妈妈，你累了！
别再操心，乖乖地睡吧！
有我在，你想睡就好好睡吧！』
母亲终于喘了一口气，
在我怀里睡着了。

那晚我紧抱着母亲：
『妈妈宝贝，你寂寞了！
今晚我不离开。
仔细听你一遍遍唠叨。』
母亲沉沉地睡去了。
当我千呼万呼，
再也没能唤醒母亲时，

无助的我，只感觉天塌了！
我用热泪和体温，
试图将她渐渐发冷的身体焐热。
苍天无助。神不显灵啊！

母亲，你安心睡吧！
今晚我陪你。
母亲，你怕黑暗，怕孤独。
今晚起我永远给你点上长明灯！
你不用再害怕，
也不必再担心。
明亮的灯照你去天堂，
父亲正在天堂口等你！

母亲，从今晚起，
你睡在我梦里，永不分离！

江山不老　美人依旧

南方。四季如诗
楚国有瑰宝，诗圣屈原
离骚楚辞风韵压千秋
留青史两千三百年
少时。灯下细诵
似肝胆相照
心升皎洁明月
梦境。有神来之笔
云里泼墨酿诗篇

国破家亡美人亦迟暮
屈原魂流汨罗江
撒向人间千年还有泪
惹华夏人惊梦祭奠
意在招魂归来
岁岁年年

斗转星移楚乐悠悠
门下子歆笙歌起
轻吟楚语一声
『月儿好看』
仙乐般美妙
拨动了芈月的心弦

路漫漫其修远兮
子歇马不停蹄追寻
只为那一份清清的纯情
秦国长安相约恨晚
错失一生的守候
痛了千年山河
似曾相识

月儿当空水如镜
小月儿有泪不轻洒
红尘有爱只在弹指间
异国舞榭起绸缪
曾几何时满朝尚楚风

且歌且舞且赋新诗
大秦的社稷江山
易手楚女主宰
千里铁骑呼啸平天下
万马齐喑芈月称后

千年后。寒冬
我拜谒骊山
兵马俑守灵秦宣太后
四十年文韬武略
来世后人评说
惊起鸿雁长空哀鸣

白云飘一份歉意
茫茫冬雪亦为昭世
厚厚的抽思
薄薄的惜诵

隔世英魂祈天问
何不当歌笑慰天
惜往日涉江去远游
九歌礼魂哀岁思美人
悲回风梦里几度哭春秋
醉醒后我借诗言沉浮
江山不老　美人依旧

16.08.0

辑五

动心的那一刻

惊梦

花园里一只叫春的野猫
发情叫得撕心裂肺
惊了我的美梦

梦里我与你在云里飘浮
白云将你托在天边
我在云里梦你
云雾中我们洒脱看人间

风和日丽万物复苏
天堂鸟在飞天

梦将我们带到白云之中
云蒸霞蔚湮灭灵魂
忘却尘世虚名

那只叫春猫惊了我的梦
我将美梦丢在云里
夜半起床看猫

天书

意外使偶然
颠覆成难忘的岁月
淹没在情感的沼泽中

茫茫宇宙中
我们的邂逅
是上苍的恩慈

史前无迹象的生命

从此开始繁衍
憧憬起未来

此岸望彼岸
无言无字
心灵在同一波段
将等待和盼望
写进月色
写进黎明

沉默是为了更深的期盼
它将爱拉得更缠绵漫长

即使到老
也会追忆
曾经的心跳和感伤
从诚实的眼睛里
倾泻出柔情
从完成的作品中
阅读属于我们的文字

那些逝去的令人怀念的时光
被我们写成一本本古书
它记载着夜晚和黎明
带来的悲痛与欢乐
梦幻又真实

代代相传

这是我们留下的遗赠
最珍贵最写实的天书

冥想

飞越天际
与永恒拔河

子夜
古老的星光
永不消褪的希望
在我疲惫的心田住下

三更

中天的弦月
将倒影留在湖中
烟雾里飘来你的气息

推醒朝曦
留不住梦境

今夜难眠

爱人，我今夜难眠
只因星光太灿烂
星星数着我心灵的乡愁
长久牵挂而不愿离开
惊碎了千年的来世今生
我只能虔诚地祈祷
背叛着阳光下的抱负

爱人，今夜不再有梦
只因月光洒下的相思泪
硬是滴在我的眼里

整夜凉着我的心
灵魂无法逃避月光的缠绵
生命中不可承受的轻
被深邃的天空驾驭

爱人，今夜将无眠
消瘦的月亮疼了忧郁的心
迟暮的诗魂找不回天分
红尘世界嘲弄我庄严的悲凉
爱情是刻在我身上的符号
我用尽一生捉摸你
输光了自己依然没抓住爱

回归大地

爱人，今生与你相遇
长路不再寂寞
千山万水的跋涉
你的追求在天之外
诗人一生等待只是瞬间

爱人，我灵魂的伴侣
岁月中有你的痕迹
世俗的炫耀显得苍白

梦醒后洗尽铅华
红尘的奢靡已成过眼云烟

爱人，浪迹天涯的旅途
你说过相约与我走完
渐行渐远已到血染夕阳
来一段人生探戈怎样
纵使留不住青春
誓言是否还能永恒

爱人，带着我们的诗
一起飞向天鹅座的行星
将地球亘古的传奇

在另一天体上虚拟延续
抛给人类的情感债务
终于赤裸着还给了清白的大地

天老地荒

长路与天涯能否交织
天老地荒有多久远
情感的债务能否清点
人生的轨迹何处了

在岁月的缝隙里生存
不经意已到了风卷残云时
陈年往事在幽暗中泄露
灵魂的安宁中还存放着感动

那是我见证的爱恋
何等的壮观和震撼
金星与木星约会
等待了多少个光年
为那相会的缘分

当木星在浩瀚苍穹下
向金星示爱那一刻
人类是多么渺小和苍白
我守候了一生
只为看到这奇观

一个神奇的夜晚

所有星星都在天河中布局
金星用尽全身光泽
开始向木星闪烁
那一刻的坚持
完成了伟大的使命

在万千光年中
仅为此瞬间的相遇
穿越了星空
孤独了明月
洗礼了人类的扭曲

我们的秘密

没有人理解
痛得心碎
就这样藏起来
长路与天涯较劲
走到底定是光明的天堂

深夜有感

有一份爱恋
似揉碎了芬芳的鲜花
早已在虚无中凋谢

有一种失去
恰如生离死别
要用尽余生去追悔

回望极致的一生

只剩透明的空气相随
那些人间世事早已悄无声息

有意去忽略过往细节
我的心事竟被吹出胸口
今夜我渡不到人生的彼岸

岁月已黄昏

当我们老了
你是否还记得
曾经相爱的地方
那是我们约定的天堂

当我们老了
你是否还记得
曾经做过的美梦
那是你我遥远的记忆

当我们老了
你是否还盼望
我还能为你写诗
写出当年的激情和诱惑

当我们老了
你是否还等待
清晨我给你唇边
送去的第一杯热茶

想着过往就已迟暮
当时的离别有多为难
可一个爱字能将心穿透

事过境迁我们仍无法释怀

我仰头看白云飘浮
心灵深处有一份忧伤
轻轻地，挽着浮云梦幻
梦醒后却到了生命的终点

你我见与不见
今生是真是幻
留着去那约定的天堂
一生一世慢慢说明白

动心的那一刻

春季花丛中，彩蝶纷飞
蓝天下，自由自在
翩跹起舞，成对追逐
彼此动心的那一刻
天空由它们拥有
生命之旅尽在飞舞中
那一刻，短暂美丽
动心的那一刻

在花蕊中瞬间释放
似生命以极限至永恒
完成了爱的使命
告别了眷恋的天空
留一世风流
万紫千红染人间

这般感人的付出
千万年后我们似彩蝶
那一刻，自由飞舞

品茶人生

致老友安德鲁

夏日夕阳疲惫地沉落时
我品着清晨留下的一杯陈茶
纯正的陈年大红袍
既带山岩的厚重甘苦
亦不缺陈皮兰花之柔甜
留在舌尖及唇间
绕有几分感悟
思绪随茶香聚散

我亦品味这人生陈茶
前世飘浮。寻五味俱全
后生沉静。聚精华满园
人生陈茶品的是气度风骨
更品具深涵的人格魅力
最后留下的那一杯
该是茶韵的灵魂
纵然它已色泽暗淡

后记

继二〇一三年诗集《中国红》《法国蓝》中英文诗歌合集由上海文艺出版社发行后，二〇一四年春在巴黎书展季又完成了《法国蓝》中法文的出版。我多了许多喜欢我诗歌的读者和诗友。真诚希望给大家写出更多好诗，写诗的欲望也越发强烈。内心深处有一份挥之不去的情怀，天空有一缕属于我的彩虹，驱使着我在诗歌创作的天空自由飞翔。白日繁忙喧嚣后，我喜欢在夜深人静时与诗倾述衷肠，梦里也常有奇妙诗句。心灵深处的情感想用诗歌向读者抒发，第三本诗集《红蓝如凌》的中英文创作也就此完稿。

诗集名的由来得益于朋友们的才智。关注我的老师、同学，诗歌和出版界的前辈、好友都希望我的新诗集与《中国红》和《法国蓝》有延续性，有我的个性和特点。白桦老师给《红蓝之恋》；有老友提议《红中蓝》；也有老同学说《红与蓝》更好。春节前我与上海一挚交聊起正为新诗集的书名纠结，他说容他想想，我知他工作繁忙，以为仅随口一说而已。岂知年初三在法国凌晨三点时，我收到他的新年问候，还建议诗集名可否题《红蓝如凌》。他觉得我名字中的『凌』字有

「凌空」「凌云」之意，且「红蓝如凌」合在一起与我的诗歌主题都十分吻合。我好生感动和惊喜，却又怕略显张扬。后当许多文化和出版界好友都一致认为此名美好贴切，非它莫属时，我才确信：就是它了！感谢好友的真诚和渊博的文学智慧！

七月底趁从巴黎回国之际，匆忙将诗稿交出版社后便感一身轻松，与家人跑到美国姐姐家休假两周，也想借此闲暇补上后记。难得休假，就放纵了一番。姐姐在新英格兰地区的青山州，顾名思义青山绿水矣！姐姐住在一名校（Middlebury College）所在小镇。她在此教中文和中国书画，教得自信，活得自在，有自己一片天地。她在花园内种满了缤纷的鲜花，还种菜种豆，自家的枫树山坡紧连小镇山峦。我每天清晨起来都喜欢先花上一小时爬一趟山。每晚在此看到的夕阳总是那么让人心动，我忙碌着还在寻求什么呢？是该慢下脚步了！坐在姐姐花园里喝香槟赏日落，那时刻那心境看着血红的夕阳变幻着色彩，触动我对人生的感悟，可就在瞬间有所思时，夕阳却彻底退下了，这使我突然伤悲起来，人生不正如此吗？无论如何眷恋这世界，总还是会逝去的，难道不是吗？

为这消失的夕阳而感伤，也无心境写后记，还是游山玩水吧。与家人开车一路游览老城，也走访大学，美国校园美丽宁静，使我怀旧和憧憬。这里的枫树漫山遍野，极其壮观。当然也就盛产枫浆、枫糖；枫木手工制品更是扬名世界。我对手工木制艺术品情有独钟，所以也一路找寻过往熟悉的枫木艺术坊。失望的是因美国经济危机，由高级木艺匠人精心设计、手工制作的艺术品少有买主，加之廉价木制商品冲击市场，不少木艺坊被迫关闭，手工木艺匠人抑或失业抑或只能去改做实用家具。我实在为美国传统匠人的随之消失、败落而感可悲。

由此而联想到：中国自古就是诗歌大国，可现代社会注重经济利益，有些青少年无心读诗。这是何等大的伤悲啊！中国诗人不也像美国匠人一样随着时代潮流而消失吗？

农历七月十五中元节那天，经过一天疲惫的游走，我们终于穿过 Stowe 镇来到山顶的『Trapp Family Lodge』，这是著名电影《音乐之声》的原型家庭留下的美丽山庄，也是电影拍摄的实景场地。从阳台上观望，真是美不胜收，我在此寻找写作灵感。晚餐喝着 Trapp 家庭喜爱的奥地利皮诺白和梅露红葡萄酒并享用家族传统的奥地利大餐，所有蔬菜瓜果，家禽畜牧都由山庄自种自产，美味无比。再跳起奥地利圆舞曲和探戈，别样情调……深夜尽兴之后回房，窗外的月光又引领我走到阳台，明亮的圆月挂在山顶，美轮美奂。月亮对我总有特别的诱惑，它给我无限的遐想和回忆……月光照耀下的山坡，名叫『思念原野』（Longingfield）。刹那间勾起我无言的乡愁。在美国与家人一起，我在思念什么？定一定神，是啊，我不正在思念法国和故乡此时的月亮吗？习惯了浪迹天涯的我，却一生都将与乡愁为伴！美景与乡愁交织，今晚在皎洁的月光下写就了后记。

要特别感谢我的老友保罗·安德鲁，他的画作令我的诗集增色添彩。同时，也感谢骆寒超、赵丽宏两位老师，在百忙中读我的诗并为此诗集作序。令我感动之至。还要感谢陈昕、王为松两位多年挚交，没有他们的真诚帮助和上海人民出版社的努力，此诗集也难以如期问世。

最后，再一次感谢亲爱的读者们，感谢始终关爱我的前辈和朋友们，是你们给了我写诗的激情和灵感！是你们使我的心灵永远年轻和纯净！

二〇一六年农历十五中元节于美国青山州思念原野

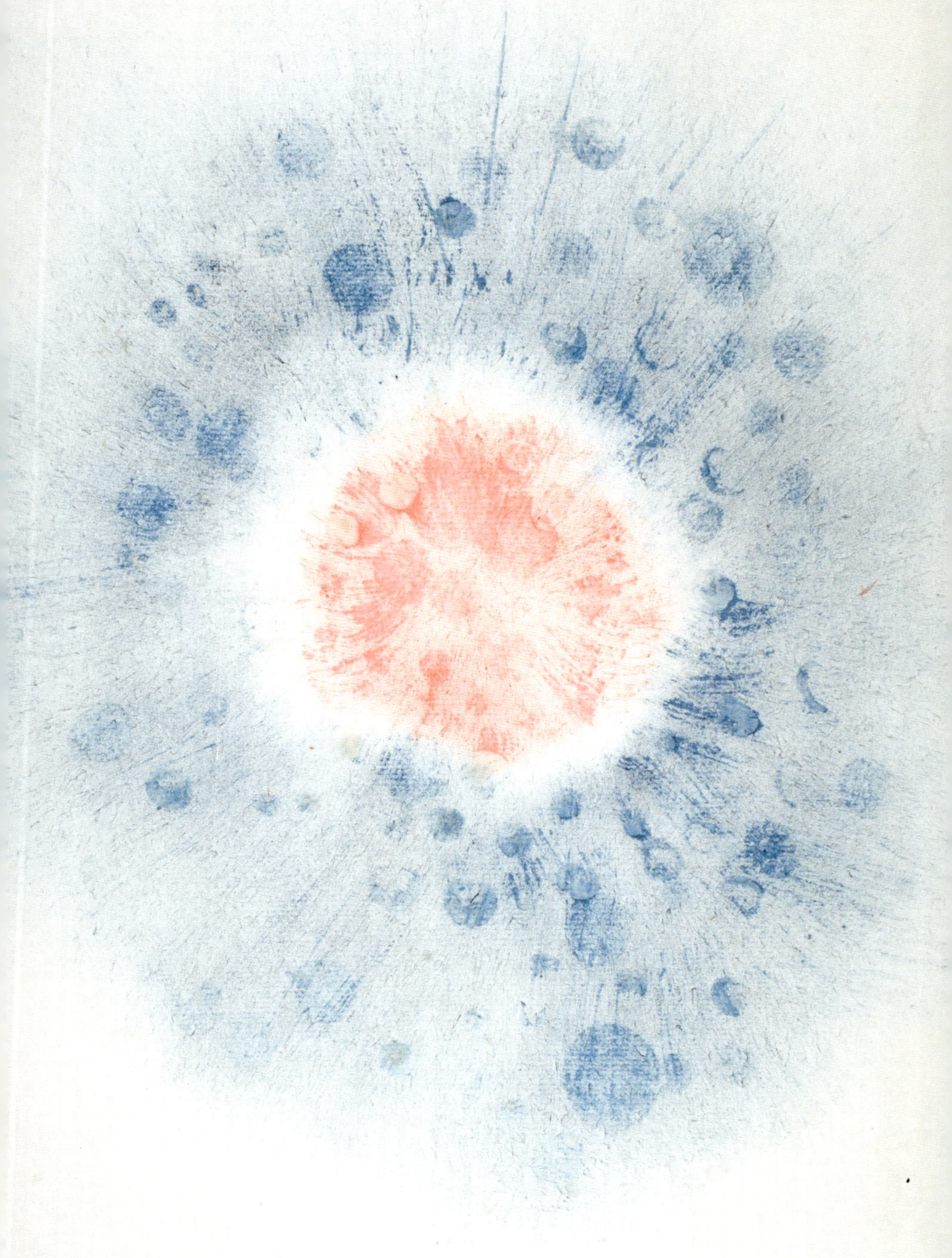

Ruling Zhang
Paintings by Paul Andreu

RED BLUE RULING

上海人民出版社

RED BLUE RULING

A POETRY COLLECTION BY RULING ZHANG

PAINTINGS BY PAUL ANDREU
EDITED BY SHU GUANGHAO
DESIGNED BY BAO CHENHUI

PUBLISHED BY SHANGHAI PEOPLE'S PUBLISHING HOUSE

ISBN 978-7-208-14130-8

To My Beloved People

Paul Andreu's painting No. 7

Akhal-teke in Her Dream

Zhao Lihong

I unfold a handful of jewels
Revealing stories held back
A gust of wind
Blows them to the sky
They turn into glimmering stars

These are the verses from Ruling Zhang's poem *I Bypass the Memory*. Poems, like jewels unfolded in her hands, are actually springing out of her soul. They fly to the sky, turning into glimmering stars... When reading such a poem, I not only admire her imagination but her confidence. There are reasons for such confidence, as the poetry book *Red Blue Ruling* in front of my eyes proves. I read through this book intermittently. When reading it, I always fell into reveries. Her poems arouse my emotions, as well as my thought.

It is unquestionable that Ruling Zhang is a brilliant poetess. She possesses not only an oriental heart but western feelings. In her poem *To Poet* she declares:" As a poet / You shall not only possess / A single piece of sky / A single stretch of land / As a rebellious poet / You shall rove all over the world / Gazing up at another piece of sky / Roaming on another stretch of land. " Growing up in the south

of the Yangtze River, the Chinese culture lays a solid foundation for her in poetry writing. Having lived in Europe for a long time gives her a broad view of western culture. In her poems, these two cultures have wonderful collisions and great combinations. *The Call of the Ancient* is a poem describing a dream that is unique in composition, profound in meaning, and with deep affection. It is a poem that leaves a lingering aftertaste in the mind of the readers. The poetess had an ancient Chinese dream at the seaside of Normandy in France. When waking up, the past and the present are integrated, the distance of time disappears:

Last night. In my dream
My dear horse left
That dark brown Akhal-teke
Along the Huan Xi River in Zhuji
A cool and peaceful Mid-autumn night
Led by holy moonlight
Towards the vast prairies in the Spring and Autumn Era
He takes the beauty Xishi away
The lady beloved by Fuchai, King of Wu
Looking for the homeland three thousand years back
Following dreams. Riding without rein
He should have gone long ago
The years belong to him
So liberal. Free from concerns

I wake up. Tears fall like raindrops
Awakened by the clatters of horses' hooves
Outside my window. A white sand beach
A seaside horse track in Normandy
Two lovers are laughing
On their Akhal-teke
They gallop away...

She talks about dreams in poems, and looks for poems in dreams. Her deep affection for the motherland, the exclamations of the past years and the longings for love, are all condensed in this short poem and conveyed by the sound of hooves. They fly over beaches and through eras, the significant meaning of the poem thrills the readers.

Ruling's poems are full of free imagination. In her *Meditation* she "flies over the skyline / contesting eternity". She travels around the world, her imagination vividly flies over mountains and seas in her verses. However, wherever she is, the motherland and her beloved ones are always the indispensable characters in her poems. She writes about nostalgia, love, the West Lake in misty drizzle in Hang-zhou, the platanus along Fuxing Road in Shanghai, the changes of years, the sadness and happiness of life. All her poems are filled with sincere love and affection. There are no shallow words in her poems. In her life, she finds inspiration and looks for poetic feelings. The images in her poems contain very profound meanings. The po-ems that express her longings, gratitude and love to her parents are extremely touching.

Ruling is not a professional writer. She has a very successful career, which makes people wonder how she manages to save energy and find time for writing. However, what I can feel from her poems is not bustle or fickleness, but a kind of serenity, a deep thinking of humanity and her love of life.

In the noisy city, she "found freed space for inspirations / and picked up lost verses along my way". She compares the ideal poems as stalactites, which must slowly grow in grottos, and as amber, which, buried deeply over millions of years, turns perfectly mellow. She refuses ordinariness, shows her personality in the poems and in her unique thinking about life. For example, *Intoxicated with the Aroma*

of Eaglewood represents her pursuit. In her poem, the aroma of the eaglewood is surprisingly out of "An emotional disaster / Hurting all over / Pain / Impossible to remove". Its "virtue of pride" is touching as it is "the misshapen aesthetics, a cruel intoxication". Such imagery and deep thoughts are the distinctive findings of Ruling.

A very short period of time is a theme frequently appearing in Ruling's poems. Or we may say, it is an eternal theme underlying her writing. A poem named *Too Late*, is a wonderful poem about this theme, and different readers may have different feelings about it. Time passes for everyone. What does it leave? Ruling gives her extraordinary feelings in the verses:

Your familiar calls were in my dream
I trotted forward in anxiety
Too late to hold hands as you bade farewell

I dreamt of you knocking at my door
Wrinkles carved in your smile
Too late to touch you before you leave

Written in Four Steps Study in Shanghai
August 14th, 2016

Poetry is the Pure Land of the Heart

Luo Hanchao

I got to know the poetess Ruling Zhang purely by chance. The senior poet Bai Hua recommended a set of poems to the poetic periodical Galaxy for which I worked. Those poems written by Ruling all about love were fervent, sincere, and twinkling with the beauty of purity. It was obvious that the writer was talented at writing poems, so we published the contributed poems. Later she sent me two poetry books *China Red* and *French Blue* in a Chinese-English bilingual edition. From then on I knew that she was a Chinese French person, who accomplished her highest studies in modern poetry at the top universities in the United States and France, and later worked in the field of architecture in Paris. It is unusual for a Chinese girl to strive abroad over 30 years to be a successful professional woman, and be awarded by the French Government the Chevalier de l'Ordre National du Merite and then the Officier de l'Ordre National du Mérite. She could have led a comfortable and easy life abroad, but she didn't! Due to the responsibilities of her work, and especially because of her longing for her motherland, she returns to Shanghai frequently. She may wander along Fuxing Road, or intone by the Huangpu River.

She wrote those two books of poetry from her overlapping cultures of China and the West. Her love and longing for China and France are combined. The touching emotions provide the distinctive flavour to Chinese contemporary poetry. I am deeply moved by what she has accomplished in her poetic work.

Ruling visited Hangzhou not long ago. We had tea and talked in high spirits at the shore of West Lake. She handed me a pile of printed poems, saying that she was preparing to publish her third poetry book, and would like me to write a preface for her. So I was honored to be the first reader of this poetry book *Red Blue Ruling.* After I finished reading the poems, I felt deeply that Ruling's new poems have original content, and that her writing skills have greatly improved. Naturally, I decided to write something for her.

The name of this new poetry book, *Red Blue Ruling*, suggests that Ruling has a new intention to integrate the fervent and bright "China Red" with the elegant and serene "French Blue". The expression of her emotions is comprehensive. They are about the longings for her homeland when traveling around the world, and for the modern love and the harmony of hearts. It seems right that I get this impression simply from the book name, since the most impressive part of the poetry book to me is how Ruling tells her feelings about human affection along with her expression of nostalgia from her global view. It is worth mentioning that an interesting logical expression is hiding in this book: love and affection must lead to harmony, and harmony is the sublimation of love and affection; the love to motherland must lead to nostalgia, and nostalgia is the sublimation of the love to motherland. Such logic of emotional expression shows that the poetess is fond of the purity of life, which is clearly reflected in poems *Returned to the Earth*, *Years at Dusk*, *Should You Allow* and *Along the Spring River on a Moon Night.*

Let us take a look at *Returned to the Earth.* This is a poem in which the heroine speaks to the beloved of her eternal love: "My love, the

trip to the sky's edge / You promised to bring me along". But when they are "receding in the blood-red sunset", can they still "dance the tango of life"---let the youth circulate just like waltz? Of course not. Although it is impossible to "extend the youth", "our oath" can be kept forever. This is the sublimation of love and desire---they just want to love each other and share the harmony of souls. But it is not enough. The imagination develops further in the poem, the heroine wants to "take our poems," to "fly to the planet of Cygnus" with her lover. Their "ancient legend" will perpetuate in another star, while their bodies shall be "finally returned bare to the innocent earth". "The body born pure is buried pure"---it is a harmonious pursuit of life to the earth that gives people an impassioned and noble feeling. Such pursuit in *Years at Dusk* is even more touching.

The love poems cover a big part of this book; they are chanting for the desires of life. In fact, they could be regarded as a noumenal symbol that symbolizes the wish for a harmony of the flesh and the spirit including that of the human beings. The existence of the logic of emotional expression also reflects the poetess' deep affection for the world, which is also remarkably shown in the poems *Platanus in Autumn*, *Wasting Time in Late Autumn*, *Release the Soul of this Life* and *A Night Visit at West Lake*. In *Release the Soul of this Life*, Ruling says that she has "a spiritual pursuit", like "waiting in loneliness for a thousand sails passing". What is she pursuing? It is "the moon from home" when "looking at the sky from a lane deep in the old town".

It is also the love of the land when a strange place has finally become a new home after going through "clouds and rains of eight thousand miles". But when she has travelled "eight thousand miles" again to her homeland, and walked into the old mansion to relieve her homesickness, she feels only emptiness when she leaves. The old home in China doesn't exist anymore; her real home is beside the remote Seine River. "Years flow without notice; clouds float

without a trace", the traveler "I" shall "bid farewell"---to the new home.

However, are "the new buildings and villas" able to "release the soul of this life"? To a passionate poetess, everywhere in this broad world could be her home, could stimulate her love for it; but the home will always turn into a strange place later; that's why her nostalgia never ends. These are the delicate and bright expressions from a world traveler who possesses a deep love for the world and never stops her spiritual pursuit. Such expressions in *Platanus in Autumn* make the readers think deeply.

In addition to the above poems, I would like to mention one that is unforgettable to me: *The Call of the Ancient*. At midnight, in my dream, an Akhal-teke took the beauty Xishi at the Huangxi River under Mount Miluo and galloped into the Spring and Autumn Era, which was three thousand years ago. They were trying to find again her husband Fuchai, the king of Wu, and retrieve the lost homeland…but I woke up then. When my "tears fell like raindrops", "I" heard the clatter of the horses' hooves and saw:

Outside my window. A white sand beach
A seaside horse track in Normandy
Two lovers are laughing
On their Akhal-teke
They gallop away...

This is a wonderful thought that combines the harmony of love and affection with the longings and nostalgia for homeland, a remarkable thought that turns the history from heroic into harmonious and the people from nostalgic to longing. And this is an ecological chorus of the global village that finally heads to harmony.

Now we can hear the sincere words from the heart of this Chinese-French poetess who travels around the world with her deep

affections: fervent and serene, delicate and bright.

I am glad to know from *the Call of the Ancient* that Ruling has evolved from her old writing style that purely expresses her feelings whenever she is touched. Now she is trying to express her feelings from outside to inside based on her real life. It is completely new to her. In this poem, her artistic conception contains time and space, history and reality, the East and the West, which make this poem mythical, real and integrated. It is closely related to her feeling about the visits to the Huanxi River in China and Normandy in France. In poetry writing, pure expression of feelings is just an ordinary way of writing, which usually suits the sensitive poets, and such writing might lead to obscurity or shallowness. It seems necessary for me to pursue a true feeling of life, and advocate the change from outside to inside then to outside again. Therefore, Ruling's new way of writing is worth admiration. *In the Deepness of the Desert*, *Wasting Time in Late Autumn* and *Airborne Visitors* are very representative in this aspect. In the poem *In the Deepness of the Desert*, the poetess says, when walking in the desert and looking at the sky and earth, one could feel that "Human beings are insignificant / The lives are short". It is a true feeling from the outside world. The following two paragraphs are the supernatural imagination derived from the true feeling. In the second paragraph, "It is a world / Dead before years of the Flood"; in the third paragraph, the time in the deepness of the desert "Is free from all anxieties / Flowing here". Such imagination makes people think that the subject has entered into the deepness of time and space. The imagery of the poem lets the reader have an aesthetic taste of mystery, nobility and the ancient world. If the subject is not involved in the objective world and does not incite the true feelings of life, how can such wonderful thoughts be captured?

Wasting Time in Late Autum is, in my opinion, a complete, organic and harmonious poem. It is good because it comes out of the true

feelings of life, with very strong imagery on a higher artistic level. The poem is about Ruling who enjoyed a tranquil afternoon in late autumn after her busy work. She strings her imagination about enjoying a short time of tranquility at home into a relaxing and emotional poem. Here is a scene about admiring the garden covered by yellow leaves: "I lean against the window listlessly / Trying to catch some falling maple leaves / They are too light / I cannot catch them even with two hands". When she look up to the blue sky of Paris, it is like "Looking at the free clouds / They are floating at will / Stopping in front of me and drifting away / The scene is a little sentimental / And a little tender / A feeling of nothingness / Surrounds me". Such expressions seem so easy to acquire, so fluent to intone and so profound in meaning. It all depends on her ability to catch the true feeling from the outside image of a subject, make a combination of imagery, and then achieve its profundity. Imagery is a subject that cannot be controlled, but be felt, by receiving the aesthetic feeling stimulated by the imagery combination expressed in a poem. Therefore, imagery is in fact, a kind of experience of the receiver. In that case, generating imagery relies pretty much on the outside subject and the feelings about it. Considering Ruling's change of writing from purely telling her feelings to emotional expression from outside to inside, I may say that her new poetry book has more imagery than her former books *China Red* and *French Blue*. A sentence "it has been long since this feeling" has occurred twice in the poem *Wasting Time in Late Autumn*. It is actually her desire to have such a tranquil and leisure life. She creates a lot of imagery for the readers, so that readers are able to experience the strong and floating beauty of imagery.

It is worth mentioning that Ruling's change in writing also reflects her interest in closely observing the objective world. More specifically, she should be praised for she is able to put her inspiration in criticizing malpractices, such as the poems *Untruth*, *Airborne*

Visitors and so on. And I think one more important meaning for Ruling's connection abroad is that she absorbs the writing experience of modern poetry of the outside world, and to a certain extent, she exceeds the traditional Chinese poetry writing. I don't agree with the idea about making poetry modern and fashionable, but we must admit that there are many merits of modern poetry in imagery expression. Ruling is not indulged in fashion, but she doesn't reject any good things. She tries to use different writing skills with a wide span of languages, to express the themes that are intellectual, symbolic, and absurd. We may see the traces in some of the poems in this book. Some people say that her style has changed recently. I have the same feeling. As some new styles of the modern poetry appear in her recent poems. *I Bypass the Memory*, *A Dreamy Reality* and *Words from Heart* are very successful in representing the style and skill of modern poetry. *I Bypass the Memory* is a dreamy poem that is about purifying the world. The broad and magnificent universe is to represent "I" have a spiritual obligation to "watch the changes between sky and sea". "I" want to search for the "jewels" in the blue sea, let "A gust of wind / Blows them to the sky / They turn into glimmering stars". "I" also want to clean "the heritage of the Ice Age" which "resurfaces after the avalanche"---and "Overrun by uncontrollable seaweed". At the end of the poem, she raises an intellectual idea:

Thousands of years flash in the blink of an eye
The last line of defense I keep
Is just the one connecting sky and sea
An instant of eternity

Yes, an instant is eternity. The eternity exists in an instant! Such expression gives people a great intellectual understanding. The pursuit of such intellectual understanding of modern poetry is of refined

taste. We could know that Ruling is not fond of playing meagre skills, nor showing off.

It is certain that the recent poems of Ruling have many remarkable words, which leave imagination to the reader, such as "The nightfall contains mature sentiments" (*Dawn and Sunset*), "The uncatchable lightyear is my destiny" (*A Swan Song through the Ages*), "When the last twilight / Licked off the tears of my soul" (*A Lonely Soul*), "The moonlight poured its perfect loneliness" (*A Night Visit at West Lake*), etc. The chapters are carefully arranged, such as *Years at Dusk, A Call of the Ancient*. Some poems are very delicate in creating a combination of images, such as *in Sleepless Tonight*: "The gloomy heart pities the emaciated moon". The moon is "emaciated" and the heart is "gloomy". Her use of metaphor to express imagery is great. Generally speaking, Ruling has worked hard on her recent poems. Just like what she writes in *Words from Heart*: "Subverted words and dissipated details / A clean soul burnished from enduring hardships / This is a lifelong thought from my heart".

How divine it is! This poetry book reaches a higher level in art. Maybe someone will ask: "Why is Ruling Zhang so fond of poetry?" Look at what she says in *A Dreamy Reality*:

Poetry is the pure land of my heart!

Written in Qiushi Village, Zhejiang Province
Aug 12th, 2016

Contents

Part One A Lonely Soul

Part Two A Late Blossom

Part Three Intoxicated with the Aroma of Eaglewood

Part One

A Lonely Soul

Paul Andreu's painting No. 8

Red Blue Ruling

Through the white clouds in the blue sky
I have gotten used to free-flying
Whatever the ending will be
The height has already been set

Looking down from the sky
Mountains are not that high
Oceans are not that broad
I carry the sunlight
Let my imagination fly with the clouds

Piercing through clouds and mist
Such a boundless sky, I sigh
A colourful rainbow
Leaves red shining with blue
My thoughts gallop along with them…

I scissor off the last beam of sunset
Inserting it between pages of poetry
It floats with the soul
Red and blue crossing the sky
Leaving a pure heart
Either engraved on people's minds
Or fading away from memories

Words from Heart

——To Poet ZHAO Lihong

Stalactites growing in dark grottos
Only one centimeter in a hundred years
Finally to be treasured by the world

Amber buried deeply over millions of years
Its colour and luster turn perfectly mellow
Finally to be favoured by the collectors

Looking for weathered glacier valleys
Only time brings great changes to the world
The earth could fulfill this ancient promise

Poems left by poets
Only those widely spread for a thousand years
Could remain embedded as classics in times

Subverted words and dissipated details

A clean soul burnished from enduring hardships

This is a lifelong thought from my heart

If you are able to listen

The world will always be a tender month of April

To Poet

Poet
Stop wallowing
Listen to me
You shall not be forgotten

As a poet
You shall not only possess
A single piece of sky
A single stretch of land

As a rebellious poet
You shall rove all over the world
Gazing up at another piece of sky
Roaming on another stretch of land

As a romantic poet
You shall extend your arms widely
To embrace the star lights of the night sky
To enjoy the broadness of the universe

As a sentimental poet
You shall stop collecting sorrows
Lamenting on your own wounds
Enough! Your writings crystallise

As a sensitive poet
You shall dignify my love
Before dawn I will disappear
Leaving illusion for the dark night

As a poet already
You shall hurry to find back
The lost years of yonder
The vanishing crescent

Poet
Stop feeling lost
Listen to me
You are inextinguishable

Should You Allow

Poet
Looking into your profound eyes
I forget my own grief
I wish to share your sorrows
Just because I understand you
Should you allow

Poet
Looking into your melancholic eyes
I dare not worry you any more
I wish to read you in my life
Just because I respect you
Should you allow

Poet
Looking into your passionate eyes
I abandon my past wanderings
Let me accompany you for the rest of my life
Just because I love you

Should you allow

Poet
Looking into your wise eyes
They see into my mind instantly
Let me love you dearly when you get old
Just because I cherish you
Should you allow

The Soul of Poetry

——To senior poet LUO Hanchao

You hold up the clouds for the blue sky
I see the remote distance
Trying to go through the space of imagination

You lit up the stars in the darkness
Hopes grow in the endless nights
And dreams stretch along infinite mountains and rivers

You grant me a piece of paper
Leaving countless suspense
The desire of writing gallops in the wildness

In between the verses
You've left blanks for me
It is your soul calling me

In every poem I write
You make your mark
Inspiring the poetic framework

Deep in the night
You turn away
Leaving a poetic trace in the stars

Before the dawn arrives
I pick up the essence of your vivid words
Sculpting and polishing marvelous verses in cadence

Spring flowers and autumn fruits appear in a blink
Rhyme and rhythms, lights and shades hopping across the lines
Are the Arias left by the past worn souls

A Lonely Soul

When the last twilight
Licked off the tears of my soul
The old and dim streetlights
Lit in position instantly and punctually
Naked, provoking me
Like drooping yellow breasts
Foretelling their senility
As they have been for years

Love distance defined by forefathers
My shadow was repeatedly
Kissed and abandoned
I couldn't find my way home

Love was exposed for too long
It was worn out
Some glistening verses
Should be inlaid on the wordless sky
Like traces of collision and attraction

Love was squandered too much
It was mottled
Going through the desolation of emotion
The wild goose in the silent night sky
A strong tearful cry
Stroke my lonely soul

Afresh, I name love
Slow down the adagio of the Nocturne
My singing under the streetlight
Almost perfect, with telepathic souls
Adding some mature years
I could faintly hear your vow
Although sky stands between us
It is engraved in my soul

Along the Spring River on a Moon Night

——Inspired by the Kunqu Opera

Stepping onto the stage
We shined in a breathtaking glory
A whole life of performance
We played many roles
In such a vivid and delicate manner
Life is a play, the play of life
We came through

It was our time
Don't you remember?
All those heroic characters
Singing powerful lyrics
Impressing the audience to a shake

These moments were real
How could we forget?

Floating lightly
With longing affections
Deeply moving the people

Posing onto the stage
Waves of unending applause
For we had so many admirers
When the show was on
They wept emotionally all along
Tender hearts touched by lingering songs
Because we played with our hearts
Performing like true life
We were the real stars

Every show comes to an end
One last time now to play the leads
We meet tonight in the show
Along the Spring River on a Moon Night
If our love lasts into the next life
We should still perform together

This is our ultimate pursuit
This is our best pose in life

The show finally ended
On the stage of life
We were hand in hand
Solemnly answering the curtain calls
No more entangled in this life's fetters
For true love never fades
Destined to cross paths in our next life

I Saw My Father Again

A restless summer night
Water has overflown the banks of the Seine River
Being alone and feeling nostalgic
I saw my father again at midnight…

My dream went back to thirty-five years ago:
After embracing the family and waving farewell
On the plane to San Francisco
I opened that small red satin-covered notebook:
"To my little girl"
auty Rem
A book of precepts my father wrote over night
A poetry book to his daughter
The only gift he had ever given to me
I read again and again in tears
His personality and honesty
Were so vividly revealed in these lines

In the dream, his verses were lingering in my mind
I wrote down: "My father---
An enlightened young man from a Christian family in Shanghai
To save the Chinese nation he pursued his ideal to Yan An
Such a belief, such a faith
Always loyal through his rugged life."

Then, I dreamed of that scene again
At Stanford, my sister visited me
She told me that our father was gone, unable to wait for me
I couldn't believe it. Really couldn't
I cried loudly: "Daddy didn't wait?
That's impossible! He promised to wait for me."
I never expected that our last farewell forever would us part

If I had known, I would have stayed with him
I should have gently touched his worn wrinkles again
I should have gazed at his smiles to me once more
No, it was not real, I was still in the dream

I was wandering along in my dream
My father was so young and handsome
Under the Pagoda Hill in Yan An
In the bright sunlight
His grin was so brilliant
I appeared there as a child
My father was on a white horse
Riding towards me, swift as the wind
Before I had time to call him "Daddy"
He had turned to Luxun Arts Academy
He was busy teaching and composing
I listened out of the cave
Awaiting him to take me home
Without noticing that he went to the bank of the Yellow River
Conducting the chorus "Delivering Grain"
Lyrics by Dada Uncle and music by my father
The song was so popular in China
How could I forget

Then, they sang “Little Peas”
“Little, little peas, bloom in purple,
My precious treasure grow up quickly.
Grow up quickly, do grow up
Join the army and beat off all enemies.”
It was a widely loved cradle-song
Composed by my dad, I learned it since babyhood
I sang with the people
Louder and better than the others
But he didn’t stay to praise me
For he rode the horse to Jin Sui Revolutionary Base already…

After that, I dreamt of him:
Having a tall hat and hanging a board
Tied up by Red Guards and forced to parade through the streets
I shouted in the crowd:
“He isn’t a capitalist, he is my dad.
He isn’t a spy of the Kuomintang
He is a patriotic fighter against the Japanese, a good person!”
I wasn’t able to shout the words again

For I was beaten and arrested
I cried loudly:
“Dad, come rescue me!”

I was awakened by my own cry
Today is thirty-five years later

So surprised when I awoke
As today is his 100-year birthday

The whole life of my father was busy
His achievements need no comments
The mountains and rivers stand witness
The sun and moon can confirm

Dear father, may you rest in peace!
Let me slowly tell your stories …

Paying Respect to Chopin, a Poet and a Virtuoso

——Fulfilled dream with son and nephew

Finally I arrived at Chopin's homeland
After half a century's waiting
Chopin's soul was still wandering
In the bright sunlight of Warsaw
Rippling streams, singing birds and fragrant flowers
It was Chopin pouring out his homesickness
The nostalgia in an instant
Could never be erased

Though he left one and a half century ago
I still heard the graceful melody of his Waltz
The brisk rhythm of his Mazurkas
The cheer and deepness of his Polonaise
And the dreamy harmony of his Nocturne

The genius of the piano, the fame he well deserved
Every melody he composed
Was a masterpiece, so vivid and idyllic
He was telling heartfelt thoughts
With profound affections and tears
About his homesickness
Facing the disintegrated motherland
With no home to return
His young and passionate heart
Was thoroughly broken

Paris took him in
George Sand's love
Healed his pain and sorrow

Inspired his passion of creation
It was the most beautiful time in his life
His nostalgia in heart
The sorrows of his nation and himself
His persistent thinking and pursuits
Were finally transformed into
His ultimate expression of love

The collision of homeland and foreign land
An excellent match of poems and music
The harmony and fluency of classic and modern

A perfect combination of technique and emotion
He accomplished to extremes
And deserved his fame
With no successors, and no predecessors before him

Yes, he was the only one
After passing in a foreign country
All of Paris held the holiest funeral
As he rests peacefully in Père Lachaise
People pay respect to him from all over the world
On his gravestone, there are sealed love letters to this day
But his ever-beating heart was returned to the homeland
He is the only one in the world
A legend who wrote poems for the piano

At Chopin's Museum in Warsaw
We played his Marche Funèbre
To memorize and pray for him
39 years old, how glorious a youth
A shining star
Never extinguished in people's heart

Part Two

A Late Blossom

Paul Andreu's painting No. 9

The Seduction of Spring

Here spring is coming
Coming too early
Coming so suddenly
The world is not ready for its new wear
But nakedly she shows to the universe

Spring greets us warmly
I see the splendid colours
I listen to the flowers blooming
I smell the soil moistening
This opulence I have been long expecting

Spring is very much in the air
The earth is spreading the desire
It is so eager and riotous
Paused but started again
Spring is lascivious with fantasy

The seduction of spring
Comes directly and ferociously
It is irresistible
The love frozen in hibernation
Is completely revived

The graceful swans
Are bearing new lives
What spring means to them
Is loyalty and devotion
Purity and faithfulness

The love of humans
Stems from the seduction of spring
When the beloved ones are together
Spending time in vain is the sumptuous desire
Loving people are entitled to the privilege of spring

Misty Clouds

Top of the mountains
Wreathed with white clouds
Getting close, it's the gauzy mist
Grasp the moistened emptiness
Dropping as rain
Hanging on as inspiration
Light and fresh dreams wander around
Just let them drift and float in the sky
How nice

West Lake in Misty Drizzle

——To Madam Sylvie BERMANN*

West Lake ever sleeping
In the land of South Yangtze
Lying here for a thousand years
Flowing with the lingering charm of centuries of poets

The beauty of West Lake lies in its generosity
Embracing the mountains
Not attempting to own them
Fusional spirit with Lei Feng Pagoda
In between water and sky
Showing mutual support and understanding
Affectionate and slender willows
Bending to make up for their frivolousness

The beauty of West Lake lies in its peacefulness
Water in spring turns into exquisite affections

Breeding graceful lotus flowers
Their discreet scent in midsummer night so intoxicating
Their reflection in the water so seducing
Bright clouds of all shades and colours
Posing and boasting in the sky
The modest lake looks upward, indifferent

The beauty of West Lake lies in its reserved nature
It collects all essences of the world without flaunt
Scene of a thousand years of romance
Ripples of a hundred years of love and hatred
Haven where orioles sang in the willows
A lake of glamour left for the world
Not a flirtation
But true love

This was the West Lake I had been longing for
I arrived in a misty drizzle
Pursuing verses of Tang and Song poets

Got my feet wet to follow dreams
with my friends in poetry
Immersed again in the depth of emotions
Found freed space for inspirations
And picked up lost verses along my way
Tonight I shared my dream with West Lake

*Sylvie Bermann——Former French Ambassador to China

A Night Visit at West Lake

In my dream I have much nostalgia
Holding my broken heart
Under the tranquil moonlight
I met you at West Lake
For the Moon Festival

I seek your trace
At the place you left
Spending my lifetime to prepare for
The moment of your return
The most solemn reunion under the sky

Wandering the world only for deep sentiment
The lost years turned into the maturity
All details fade away in adversity
Prosperity and glories have gone
Let's reclaim the wasteland sincerely

I pick up your glittery poems
Hide my longings in the seasons
The moonlight poured its perfect loneliness
I settle my sorrowful heart up to the sky
The lake reflects the silhouettes of two naked bodies

Wind and Rain on West Lake

Late in a midsummer night
Visitors were all gone
West Lake became quiet

The rain kept falling
The wind kept blowing
The lake rippled gently
Amidst the rain

No home here for me
I was alone
Wandering along Su Causeway
My lonely heart
Committed to the wind and rain at West Lake

Rain has no home
Wind has no home

And I have no home

We were unrestrained tonight

Brimming the lake with secret tenderness

It was a feeling only we knew

Pattering, the rain dropped for me

Whistling, the wind blew for me

No more lonely tonight

Dawn and Sunset

The bright sunlight
Wakes up at dawn
It is full of fresh happiness
Giving off a life of seduction

Boasts to conquer
All life on earth
Keeping brightness in the sky
Shining sunlight never fades

The sun is high
Its light floods the land
But it cannot resist its fall
Leaving just a glow of blood red

With different magnificence
Dawn and sunset are at opposite ends
Graceful sunset changes every second
Signals its calm and elegant departure

The nightfall contains mature sentiments
A lasting spirit emerges in an instant
Although it is a passing traveler of the universe
Its dreams can last forever on earth

Afterglow

Late autumn. Cold dew falls
The sunset is getting solemn and heroic
Carrying its past magnificence
It seeks the desire for hibernation
We must not disturb
Nor say adieu
Beyond the sky
You will see
It never stops rising or setting

Wasting Time in Late Autumn

A sunny afternoon in late autumn
Piercing through the colourful leaves
The lights pour into the window
So willfully and proudly
My thoughts are disturbed
I cannot concentrate on my writing any more

Clouds drifting across the sky of Paris
A rare sunny Sunday
Just let me indulge
It has been long since I had this feeling

It rained the whole night
The garden outside the window
Is covered with yellow leaves
I lean against the window listlessly

Trying to catch some falling maple leaves
They are too light
I cannot catch them even with two hands

Looking at the free clouds
They are floating at will
Stopping in front of me and drifting away
The scene is a little sentimental
And a little tender
A feeling of nothingness
Surrounds me

Make a pot of afternoon tea
Savour it alone slowly
A rare peacefulness
A rare flatness

In this flat afternoon of autumn
I recall some past trivia
And cannot avoid retrospection
I waste my time vainly
It has been long since this feeling

Platanus in Autumn

The West wind blew down the last leaves of Platanus
Stepping on a carpet of yellow leaves at midnight
I walked alone on Fuxing Road
It was quiet at night
So was my heart

All vanities fading
I listened to the sound of leaves falling
I breathed in the lingering aroma
Reflecting on the elusive autumn day
And the traces of the past years

Until now I couldn't remember
How many times I walked along Fuxing Road
How many times I trod on Platanus leaves
It is a memory I am very fond of
Whether at home or abroad

The Platanus brought me nostalgia

I followed my childhood dream

To the place of its origin

The fallen leaves flourished with emotions

As they fell down to an unknown place

A Late Blossom

This long winter
After hurting my heart
Finally discarded me
The ambiguous spring
Comes late and miserly
Noble and pure the magnolia
Unable to resist
A hailstorm in early spring
The flower looked weary
Yet withered so early

In the fine spring days
The pink and glorious cherry blossom
Burst willingly
Affectionate and attentive
So real, so rare
But blown by a well-contented wind
Only maintaining a flimsy look

Petals fall down
Making me feel much sorrow
I bury them with tears in my eyes
For her fate and also my own

The tulip is delicate and dotted
The florescence too short to show off
I wish I could admire longer
But she withers resignedly
What a doleful end
An empty branch provides no comfort

When the colourful flowers bloom in my garden
Spring rains drizzle day and night
They pour for days
Then stop after a good time
Washing away the innocent charm of spring

The humble violet lilac
Successfully bearing loneliness
Now has a chance in spring
To release her weak endurance
Blossoming at will
Yet unable to compete with others
This tiny bud
Draws my attention
Blossoming boldly and freely
The fragrance sways the garden
And finally fills my heart

When the lilac is in full blossom
The tale of spring begins
Now I am full of tenderness
To wait for your late return

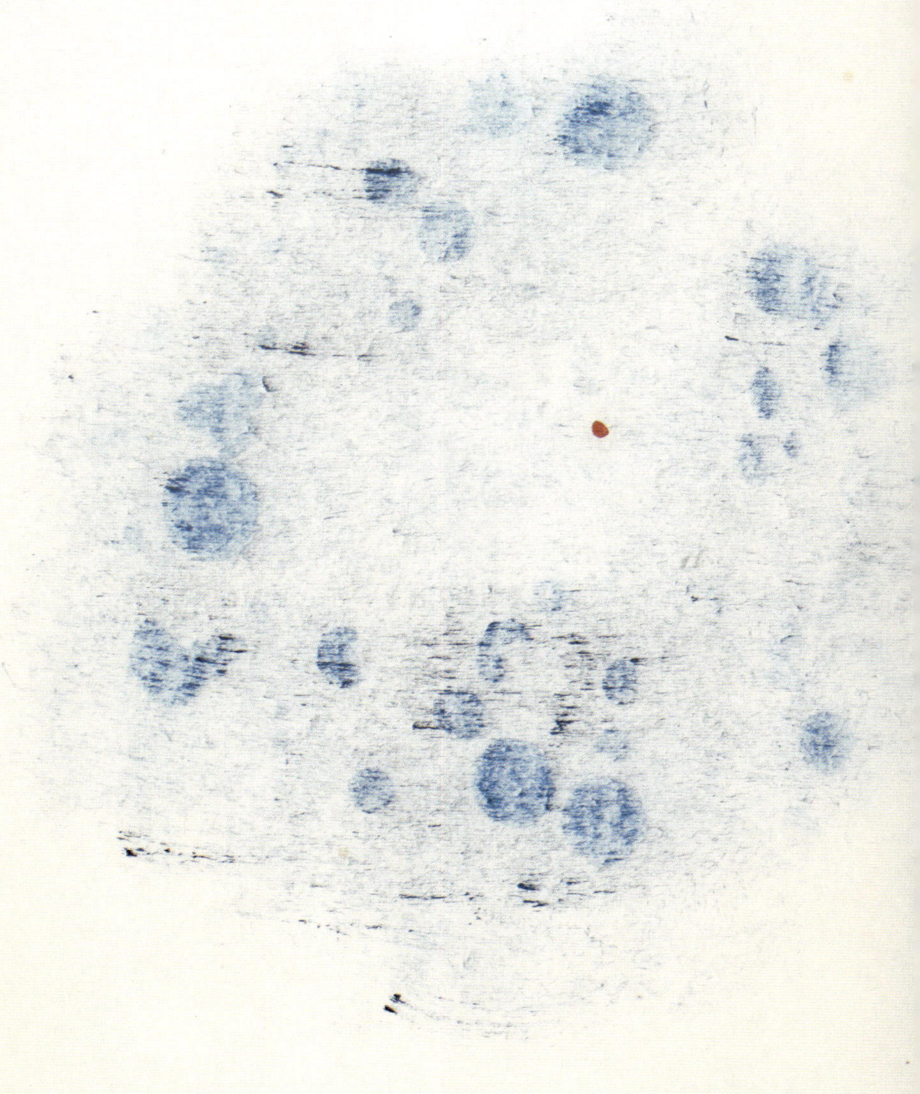

Part Three

Intoxicated with the Aroma of Eaglewood

Paul Andreu's painting No. 10

Intoxicated with the Aroma of Eaglewood

An emotional disaster
Hurting all over
Pain
Impossible to remove

Burnt some old crumbs of eaglewood
The slowly rising smoke
Dreamily fascinating
Dispels my heart's sorrow and pain

Intoxicated with the aroma of eaglewood
I am moved by its virtue of pride
Only once parasitized by fungi
Could the balm finally be left to the world

Heavy is the eaglewood
A life long enough
Thought to be few and far between
So rare is the wood in this world
Used as a soothing pain-killer and a scent

Heavy is the eaglewood
Rotten for a thousand years
Shaped like dried off rocks
Collected as treasure
From ages ago

Such misshapen aesthetics
What a cruel intoxication

In the Deepness of the Desert

Walking in the desert
I look around the sky and the earth
Human beings are insignificant
The lives are short

The desert lying in eternal peace
Sleeps soundly for millions of years
It is a world
Dead before the years of the Flood

What we question and pursue
And the time we then neglect
Is free from all anxieties
Flowing here

I enjoy feeling the desert

Tirelessly writing epics for the human
About our centuries-old love stories
When finishing one page
I hide it secretly
Then I write the next page
Diligently and ceaselessly

I bury the written epics
Deeply in the desolated desert
After thousands of years
Those moving chapters
Arising like mirages
Astonishing heaven and saddening ghosts
Become ancient weathering ruins
They were awaiting posterity to portray
These touching legends

I Bypass the Memory

At night Pegasus flies
I bypass the memory
Gazing at the sky

Above the blue sea
A gate favours me
Leading me to a secret garden
I unfold a handful of jewels
Revealing stories held back
A gust of wind
Blows them to the sky
They turn into glimmering stars

Between sky and sea
Is the distance separating you and me
It is so close
As if within a hand's reach

It is so far away
Unreachable up the ladder of heaven

The heritage of the Ice Age
Resurfaces after the avalanche
Floating and breeding in the sea
Overrun by uncontrollable seaweed
The sea shall be held hostage
Forbid its flirtations
Dry off all waters
Sever all temptations
For the sea to turn clean

I bypass the memory of billions of years
Only watch the changes between sky and sea

Thousands of years flash in the blink of an eye
The last line of defense I keep
Is just the one connecting sky and sea
An instance of eternity

Untruth

The arid hot summer
Lies rattled on ceaselessly
Accusing the straight oak trees
Inventing fragmented details
Into growing inflorescences
Falling quickly and prematurely

On the lake that summer
Leaves fell in a panic
Filled with withering despair
The poppies look like violet lip prints
Caressing the lake where memories are forgotten
Sublimating the soul before sinking

Just overnight
A sealed virginity was stolen
The evil chaos in people

Controlled the situation

For some petty profits

I was involved in a fictitious story

Retrieving dignity in the rays of sunset

I caught some voracious fish

By letting them go

They appreciated my mercy

In their seven-second memory

How preciously commendable

A Dreamy Reality

Rippling on the dreamy lake
I tried hard to find the memories
The accent of hometown in my dream
Aroused my nostalgia
Awoke me from my dream

Indulged in the inspiration of writing
In my most serene state of mind
Poetry is the pure land of my heart

Someone distorted the history
Even under the bright sun
Underhand means
Arose just in a moment of illness
Walking along the ruins left by the ancestors
To find the gossiping rubble
Only moved some debris
But hurt one's own body
It is the soul that needs rescue
How can one judge morality with a polluted soul

You do not understand my thoughts
Love supports me in the past and the present
You do not understand my nostalgia
Endless desires are contained in my loneliness
You do not understand the wealth of my soul
In the universe I have collected
Memories which cannot be taken away

The flood turned into a disaster
The poetry books washed away
Forgotten thereafter
An angler at the lakeside
Hooked them up
Dried them on the fishing rod
And read page after page
He found jewels from another planet
Glittering like gold
The news was ubiquitous
People rushed to be in the frontlines
To pursue treasures out of this Earth
In the marvels of Venus' revolving path

A Coming Storm

Dirty souls
In a country of freedom
Obtain their legal pass
In the narrow aisle
So crowded and messy
Fighting for their own interests
They hurt each other badly
I cannot give in and get along
So I make way for them

Distorted humanity
Hoarding greed and hatred
Exposed absurdly
But they still boast without shame
Claiming to retrieve their dignity
Referring to the simple wealth of the past

Visions are lost for thoughts are wrapped in satin
Laws are ignored when pursuing extravagance

After the brilliance the world returns to chaos
The sky is filled with falsehood
I am stunned and puzzled
Decadence of an era or fatigue of morality

I sense a coming storm
That will baptize the human conscience

Airborne Visitors

A tiny island in the Mediterranean
The white beach under the sky
A heaven for skinny dippers
The only peaceful land left in France
Untainted till now
A beam of sunshine
Cast on the sea
Nature-loving swimmers
Amidst beauty pageants
Showing their care in return

Suddenly flew down five Dolphins*
Loud noise broke the peace
Flying sands filled this square of land
The whole island was trembling
They are huge and luxurious
Coming violently
I know where they were made
In local city Marseille

A group of strangers came to the island
To worship the sea

Before their compatriots arrive
They set foot on this wonderland
All convey a sense of flashy gold
Stunning the blondes on the island
Who are these celestial beings
Landing here for a long stay

Owning the most expensive villas
Flipping clouds and shifting rain
Organic food and drinks
Fresh air and blue sky
This free and charming island
Is their best leisure resort
No worries
And no difficult choices

I speak their language

The new migrations are coming
I say to myself wordlessly

*Dolphine: A type of helicopter manufactured in Marseille

The Hunter and the Sika Deer

In a vast mountain forest
Lived a talented hunter
A stranger fond of nature

Hunting in the woods, fishing by the lakes
Nuts for food, flowers and fruit as vegetables
This kind and passionate hunter
Took care of the precious wild animals
Taught them how to escape
From dawn to twilight
A young and beautiful sika deer
Was his beloved loyal companion
True love was emanating between them

Before the cold winter came
Little deer was ready to survive on its own

And the hunter had to return to his hometown
It was so hard to part

Last time to hunt
Frost-covered fields caressed by the dawning light
The hunter was aiming at a big hare
The second he pulled the trigger
His beloved deer jumped right into his line of sight
Shot down by the hunter
Lying down on the grass, trembling
He didn't mean to hurt it

Regretting bitterly, the hunter held it tightly:
"I am so sorry, my little deer!
Tell me, why did you jump into my line of sight?"
The beautiful pure deer shed tears:

"Because of love! Do you understand?
Isn't that true?
I should have been the prey you aimed at.
Only because of your love,
Could I be so happy and free!"

"Your return day would be the time to say farewell.
Before the winter snow falls down,
The next hunter will kill me with no mercy.
I am willing to devote my life to you today,
Just because I love you so much.
Shot dead by you
What a fate I wish to pursue!"

"My adoring hunter,
At the end of my life,
Please fulfil my wish:

Bury me in your courtyard,

Let me accompany you the rest of your life.

My brave hunter,

Don't disappoint my humble wish…"

The kind hunter promised in poignant tears

The sika deer passed away in his arms…

Part Four

The Stranger at the End of the World

Paul Andreu's painting No. 11

The Call of the Ancient

Last night. In my dream
My dear horse left
That dark brown Akhal-teke
Along the Huan Xi River in Zhuji
A cool and peaceful Mid-autumn night
Led by holy moonlight
Towards the vast prairies in the Spring and Autumn Era
He takes the beauty Xishi away
The lady beloved by Fuchai, King of Wu
Looking for the homeland three thousand years back
Following dreams. Riding without rein
He should have gone long ago
The years belong to him
So liberal. Free from concerns

I wake up. Tears fall like raindrops
Awakened by the clatters of horses' hooves
Outside my window. A white sand beach
A seaside horse track in Normandy
Two lovers are laughing
On their Akhal-teke
They gallop away...

Overlooking the Homeland

——Impressions of Movie *Overlooking the Homeland*

In my dream I recalled
A beautiful island
Sandakan

I once visited the place
Where the Japanese in war
overlooked their homeland
It is a story unknown to all
The Geishas stranded for their whole lives
Looked through the ocean for their families
To survive they sang and danced
The beauty of Sandakan is sorrowful

Sandakan is still beautiful but forlorn
It makes me think of the gravestones
left by people overlooking their homeland

Too Late

The poems for you twinkled in my dream
Scattered along the way by the wind
Too late to collect but pillaged

Your familiar calls were in my dream
I trotted forward in anxiety
Too late to hold hands as you bade farewell

I dreamt of you knocking at my door
Wrinkles carved in your smile
Too late to touch you before you leave

When waking up I was old and doddering
Sharp and sophisticated in writing
Too late to portray the world as it ages

A scar deep in my heart
Never disclosed in my previous and present lives
Too late to lament as years have passed by

Release the Soul of this Life

Nobility not stemming from earth or heaven
It wanders in the soul of humans
A spiritual pursuit
Waiting in loneliness for a thousand sails passing by

True love never seeks to provoke
Nor does it share dreams with morality
Just like clouds floating, water flowing
Rolling dust cannot raise a thunderbolt

A man disregarding life and death
Could be respected or disdained
The sky doesn't care about the human world
People run after the clouds
No end after thousands of turns and twists

Looking at the sky from a lane deep in the old town
The moon from home within reach of my hands
Writing poems about clouds and rains of eight thousand miles
But only seeing emptiness when walking out of the mansion

Years flow without notice; clouds float without a trace
This world cannot accept sentimentality nor fragility
Time to bid farewell
The new buildings and villas
Are unable to release the soul of this life

The Stranger at the End of the World

Too heavy is the soul of the stranger
For your arms to embrace
Too deep are the sentiments of the stranger
For your eyes to look through
Too many sufferings has the stranger been through
For your late consolation

The stranger carries light luggage
Accustomed to traveling alone
Coming with no worries and leaving without regrets
Where can he find his soulmate?
The promises are cast
To heaven with repressed heartache

Delayed for a while
The stranger is on the road again
Disappearing at the end of the world

A Swan Song through the Ages

The winter solstice. A rare heavy snow
The banks of Huangpu all in white
Enjoying alone, filled with emotion
This scenery occurred only once in fifty years
The year we met
I looked far, longing for you

The Loire Valley. Snowflakes danced fiercely
Chambord, the palace looked magnificent
Five hundred years ago
François dedicated it to his beloved
Almost lost the throne for the Beauty
The Knight-King won his fame with a triumphant return

Spring blossoms replaced the melting ice
The glamour could not attract the hero
High walls isolated him from the war

Accompanied by his love

Never lonely

Riding and hunting in the forest

Reciting poems and pursuing dreams in the countryside

The King Architect left behind a remarkable masterpiece

The spirit of Da Vinci around the beams till now

The merits or faults are beyond judgement

The sun and the moon never meet

How many eras have the flowers blossomed in the Valley

You and I date at Chambord in our previous lives

Hunting and riding. Also reciting poems

The marvelous picturesque landscape

Makes us forget the outside world

Souls never die. Lives reincarnate

We believe in the oath of heaven

Spring comes. The next life begins
Hand in hand, Huangpu and the Loire
Death is merely a homecoming
Early April. The burning incense is delicate
So light are the ashes. So light are my poems
Burn all regrets through the ages. Make it a Swan Song
The uncatchable lightyear is my destiny
We are finally equal in heaven
What would you respond?

Mother's Orphan

Mother, you are my longing when travelling far
I am your concern for days and nights
You retain your mercy in your heart
I hold my homesickness in my hands

After you passed away
I am the orphan the homeland stopped accepting
You are above the sky
Through the clouds my mind flies up high
No expectation any more, for a reunion in the world

Mother, the affections I haven't expressed
Will be devoted to you when we meet again
This world or heaven
A thought lies between fact and fancy, in a blink

Mother Fell Asleep

Mother was tired,
Falling asleep so soundly.

That night she was in my arms,
Like a helpless child,
Looking at me weakly.
She tried to move her lips,
Yet unable to speak out a word.
I embraced her tightly:
"Baby mommy, you are tired!
Don't worry any more, have a nice sleep!"
Mother finally took a breath,
Fell asleep in my arms.

That night I hold her tightly:
"Mommy, my baby, you are so lonely!
I won't leave tonight.

I will carefully listen to your prattle."
Mother fell asleep soundly.
When I called hundreds of times,
Still unable to wake her up,
I was so helpless, only felt like the sky collapsed.
I tried to use my tears and heat,
To warm her gradually cold body.
The god didn't do me a favour. It showed no mercy!

Mother, sleep without worries!
I will accompany you tonight.
Mother, you were afraid of darkness and loneliness.
Tonight, I will light the ever-burning lamps for you!
You needn't be afraid,
Or get worried any more.
The bright lights will lead your way to heaven,
Our father is waiting for you there!

Mother, from tonight,
You sleep in my dreams, never come apart!

Land Stays Beauty Remains

South China. Poetic four seasons
Quyuan, wise master, treasure of the state of Chu
His poetry has reached the peak
Featured for two thousand, three hundred years
In my youth, diligently reading under the lamp
He was so close to me
Like a bright moon rising in my heart
In my dream. A stroke of genius
Ink-written chapters appeared in clouds

Broken country and the handsome man in his late years
The soul of the poet Quyuan flew along the Miluo River
His tears remain in the world after thousands of years
Woke the Chinese to commemorate
To invocate his spirit
Year after year

World changed but Chu's melody lasted
Pupil Zixie played the folk Sheng pipe
Singing in Chu dialect

"Girl Yue'er is beautiful"
Magnificent like heavenly music
Touched the right chord of Miyue

Along this endless way
Zixie ceaselessly searched
Merely for pure love
A regretful date so late in Chang'an of Qin
He missed his lifelong waiting
The land of a thousand years felt his pain
What a familiar feeling

Moon high in the sky and water like a mirror
Yue'er held back tears though she was sad
Love in the world vanished in a blink
Dancing in a strange country, making great plans
When the court admired the style of Chu
Singing, dancing, writing poems
The throne of Qin
Finally changed hands to the lady of Chu
Cavalry swept a thousand miles to unite the country

Horses kept silent when Miyue became the Empress Dowager

A thousand years later. In a cold winter
I worshipped Mount Li
The Terra Cotta Warriors guard the Empress Dowager of Qin
Forty years of contributions to culture and country
Let the posterity comment
Wild geese in shock crying in the sky

Clouds float with apologies
White snow as rehabilitation
Deeply concerned
Earnestly prayed

The departed great soul asked heaven
Why not sing the poems as consolation
Remember the past travels by crossing rivers
Salute souls by playing the music of Chu
In sadness I cried for the Period in my dream
When sobered up I wrote poems about the ups and downs
Land stays. Beauty remains

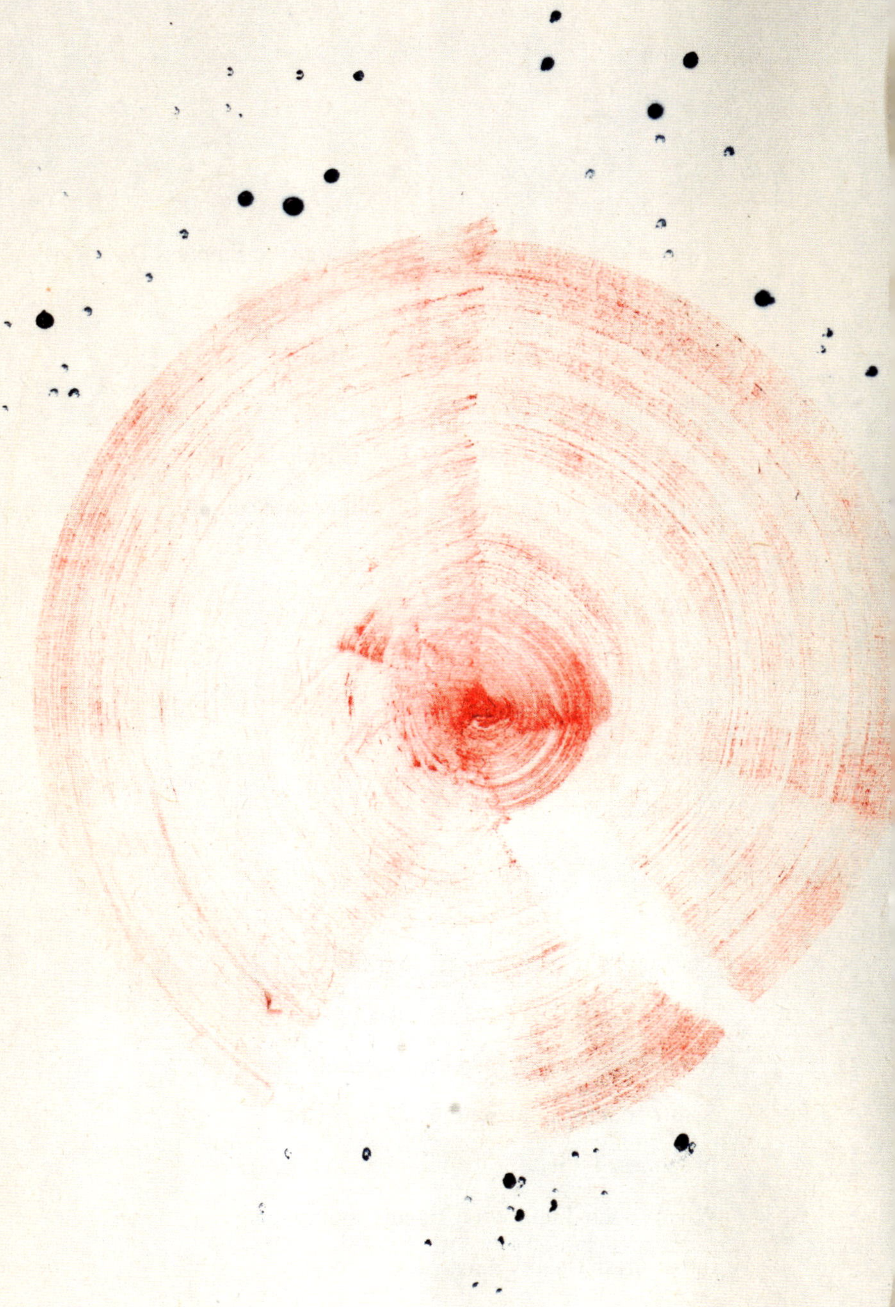

Part Five

The Instant when Hearts are Touched

Paul Andreu's painting No. 12

Dream Roused

A wild cat in the garden
Caterwauled in heat annoyingly
Suddenly disturbing my sweet dream

In the dream I flew with you in the clouds
You were held high in the sky
I dreamt of you in the clouds

We freely overlooked the world
through clouds and mist
Nature revived in gentle breeze and sunshine
We were flying like birds of paradise

The dream blew us into clouds
Our souls were drowned in rosy mist
Leaving behind dusty vanities

The caterwauling cat interrupted my dream
I lost this voyage among the clouds
Got up at midnight to find the cat

The Sealed Book

An unexpected incident made this occasion
Turned into unforgettable years
And submerged into emotional swamps

In the boundless universe
We met by chance
A benediction of Heaven

No trace of life in prehistory
Yet multiplying from then on
Longing for the future

Looking at the other side of the ocean
Untold words in our hearts
Fixed on one wavelength
Our desire and expectations
Were written into the moonlight
Written into the twilight

Silence was for deeper anticipation

It made love lasting and lingering

Even in our old age
We would still recall
The heartbeats and sentiments we had
From the honest eyes
The tenderness flows out
From the accomplished works
Our words might be read

Those past nostalgic days
Written into ancient books
Record nights and dawns
Sadness and happiness brought thereby
So dramatic but genuine
Conveyed by generations

This is our heritage
The most cherished and authentic Sealed Book

Meditation

Fly over the skyline
Contesting eternity

At midnight
The ancient star lights
Hopes never fading
Down in my weary heart

At the early dawn
The crescent shining high
Leaves the reflection in the lake
Your breath flows dimly from misty fog

The morning twilight awakens
Dreams drift away

Sleepless Tonight

My love, I am sleepless tonight
Because of the bright starlight
The stars count the nostalgia of my heart
Reluctant to leave me with long concern
Awaking the broken life of a thousand years
I could only reverently pray
Betraying the ambition under the sunlight

My love, I have no dream tonight
For the tears of longing cast by moonlight
Dropped right into my eyes
They chilled my heart the whole night long
The soul cannot elude the lingering moon
The unbearable lightness of being
Governed by the profound sky

My love, I will be sleepless all night
The gloomy heart pities the emaciated moon
At its dusk, the poetic soul has dried up
The secular world derides my solemn sorrows
Love is a deep sign carved on me
Spending my lifetime to know you
Lost myself but still failing to catch love

Returned to the Earth

My love, after meeting you
This long road, no longer lonely
Trudging for thousands of miles
Your pursuit is beyond the skyline
The poet's life-long wait is just an eye blink

My love, you are my soul-mate
Your imprints mark the years
Even the glamorous show seems pale
Washing off the vanity after waking up
All extravagance faded away

My love, the trip to the sky's edge
You promised to bring me along
Receding in the blood-red sunset
What about dancing the tango of life

If we cannot extend our youth
Can our oaths be kept forever

My love, taking our poems
Let us fly to the planet of Cygnus
The ancient legend of the earth
Will be perpetuated in another virtual star
The emotional burdens left behind by humans
Are finally returned bare to the innocent earth

When Earth and Heaven Get Old

Can the long way reach the end of the world
How far it is between earth and heaven
Can the debts of affection be counted
Where is the end of our life paths

Living through the cracks of the passing years
Inadvertently we find ourselves old and weak
The past has leaked in the darkness
In the peace of souls exists gratefulness

It is love that I witness
How glorious and powerful
The dating of Venus and Jupiter
Has gone through so many light years
Just for the fate of meeting

In the glittering sky
When Jupiter shows love to Venus
How tiny and pale are the human beings

I spend my whole life
Waiting for this wonder

In the amazing night
All stars station in the sky
Venus uses her sheen
Shining to Jupiter
The persistence of that moment
Accomplishes her great mission

In millions of years
Merely for this instant meeting
They vanish across the starry night
Leaving the bright moon lonely
Baptizing the distorted human nature

Our secrets
No one understands
They are so heartbreaking
Just hidden like that
The contest between
the long way and the end of the world
Will finally lead to a bright heaven

A Feeling Tonight

A fragment of love
Like a flower's fragrance crumbling away
Withered in nothingness

A kind of loss
Just like parting forever till death
Filled with remorse for the remaining days

Looking back on the fulfilled years
Now only attended by transparent air
All the vibrant things and people, now silent

Knowingly ignoring the past details
My thoughts gushing from my chest
Tonight I am unable to reach the other shore of life

Years at Dusk

When we are old
Will you still remember
That magic place we fell in love
It is our promised heaven

When we are old
Will you still keep
That unique dream we had
It is a remote memory we share

When we are old
Will you still wish
That I write poems for you
Full of our past emotion and seduction

When we are old
Will you still wait

In the morning for me to bring to your lips
The first little cup of hot tea

When recalling the past we feel older
How hard to be apart you and I
Heart broken, without being in each other's heart
We are not relieved though it has passed for long

Looking at the white clouds
A piece of sorrow deep in my heart
Lightly, thoughts drifting with clouds
Yet I reach the end of my life when waking up

Shall we meet or not
Is our life reality or illusion
Let us go to the promised heaven
To make it clear for a lifelong time

The Instant when Hearts are Touched

Among spring flowers, colourful flitting butterflies
Dance freely under the blue sky
They flutter elegantly, competing in pairs
The instant when hearts are touched
The sky belongs to them
Their life journey ends up flying
That very moment, so brief so bright

The instant when hearts are touched
Relieved in a blink when the buds bloom
A short life changed into eternity
Fulfilling the mission of love
Bidding farewell to the beloved sky
Their lifelong flirtation
Makes the world a splash of colour

How touching their devotion
Thousands of years later we are like butterflies
At that very moment, dancing freely

Life of Tasting Tea

——To my old freind Paul ANDREU

When the summer sun sets wearily
I am tasting a cup of tea left in the morning
The pure old Big Red Robe
With a heavy sweet and bitter flavour of rocks
And a soft sweet flavour of dried orange peels
and orchids
The taste remains on the tongue and the lips
Bringing me some feelings
My thoughts gather and scatter with the scent of tea

I am tasting the bitter old tea of life
Travelled in the first half of life
Looking for all sorts of flavours
Becoming quiet for the rest of my life

Filling the garden with essence
From the old tea of life I taste grace and strength
And even deeper the charm of personality
The last cup of tea
Should be its soul
Though the colour is getting dim

Postscript

Ruling Zhang

After my poetry books *China Red* and *French Blue* (Chinese-English edition) were published in 2013 by Shanghai Literature & Arts Publishing House, I published the French edition of *French Blue* during the Paris Book Fair in the spring of 2014. From then on, I have been fortunate that many readers and poetry friends are fond of my poems. I deeply wish to write more poems; it is a desire that grows stronger and stronger. Deep in my heart is a feeling, like a rainbow in the sky that makes me fly freely when writing poetry. After a hard day's work, late at night, I indulge myself in poetry, and magnificent verses sparkle in my dreams. I am eager to write poems to express my feelings to my readers, so I just finished my third poetry book *Red Blue Ruling*, in both Chinese and English.

I am grateful to my dear friends as the name of this book originates from their advice and suggestions. My teachers, college mates, friends and senior poets and publishers, all those who are concerned about me, suggested that the name of this book should be consistent with *China Red* and *French Blue*, and it should be true to my personality and character. The senior poet Bai Hua suggested *Love of Red and Blue*; an old friend proposed *Red in Blue* while a class-

mate thought that *Red and Blue* was better. Before the Chinese New Year, I told a good friend of mine in Shanghai that I had beaten my brains to find a proper name for my new poetry book. He said that he would think it over. I knew he was extremely busy and thought it was just a show of politeness. However, at 3 am in Paris on the third day of the Chinese New Year, I received his New Year's greetings. He asked whether *Red Blue Ruling* would be a suitable name for the book. His idea was that the Chinese character *Ling* in my name "Ruling" is associated with the expressions *Ling Kong* (high up in the air) and *Ling Yun* (reach the clouds), and he thought the combination *Red Blue Ruling* perfectly fits the themes of my poetry. How touched and pleasantly surprised I was! But I was afraid that such a name might be arrogant. When all my friends in the cultural and publishing circles unanimously agreed that this nice and felicitous name suited the book best, I was confident it should be this name! I feel so grateful to my dear friend for his sincerity and literary wisdom!

During my trip to China at the end of July, I hurried to hand over my poems to the publishing house. After that I felt relieved and travelled with my family to visit my sister in the United States for two weeks. I looked forward to finishing my postscript during this leisure period. It was very unusual for me to have a long vacation, and I enjoyed every minute of it. My sister lives in Vermont in New England, a wonderful place surrounded by green mountains and clear waters. More precisely her home is in Middlebury, famous for its college where she teaches Chinese, Chinese calligraphy and painting. She enjoys her work and life with confidence and passion, and she has a world of her own, connected to nature and her art. She plants colourful flowers and vegetables in the garden. Every early morning, I spent one hour climbing in the maple forest behind her house. Every late afternoon, I marveled at the glorious sunset. What am I busy for? Yes, it is time for me to slow down! Sitting in

the garden, enjoying the sunset with champagne, my feelings about life were touched when the blood red sunset changed colours. But the sun disappeared right at the instant of my thinking, and it made me sad. Isn't life just like that? No matter how deep one loves the world, life passes away.

Because of the sadness brought on by the setting sun, I was no longer in the mood to write the postscript. I just wanted to enjoy my vacation. We drove through ancient towns, stopped at renowned U.S. colleges, so beautiful and peaceful, making me nostalgic and longing. The most spectacular sights were the forests of maple trees, present everywhere. Maple syrup and candies are the specialties of the region and maple wood handcrafts are well-known all over the world. I love wooden handcrafts very much, but to my disappointment, many stores have closed and turned into furniture stores. Refined local artworks are difficult to sell, even more so with influx of inexpensive wooden products. I feel sad for the traditional craftsmen.

This led me to think of the current situation of poetry in China. For thousands of years, China has been a country for poetry, but in modern society it seems that the economy is more important and many young people are reluctant to read poetry nowadays. How grievous it is! Aren't the Chinese poets declining just like the craftsmen in the US?

On the 15th day of the seventh lunar month, after a long day of travel, we arrived at Trapp Family Lodge, which is on top of the mountain near Stowe, Vermont. It is a beautiful lodge built by the Trapp family, whose story is told in the famous movie *The Sound of Music*. Looking from the balcony, the scenery was so magnificent. I tried to find some inspiration for my postscript. During the dinner, we had the Austrian Pinot Blanc and Merlot wines that are favoured

by the Trapp family, and enjoyed traditional Austrian food locally produced at the Lodge. Later we had a wonderful exotic night with Austrian waltz and Tango. When I returned to my room after all these joyful moments, I was attracted by the moonlight to the balcony. The bright and round moon hung high over the mountains, graceful beyond words. The moon is very special to me, as it gives me endless imagination and arouses my memories... The slope under the moonlight is named Longingfield. My silent homesickness suddenly emerged. I was with my family in the U.S., what else was I missing? I collected my thoughts. Ah, yes. I was missing the moon in France and my homeland China. Though I have gotten used to traveling around the world, that homesickness will be my life-long companion. Accompanied by this nice scenery and nostalgia, I finished the postscript under the bright moonlight.

I am extremely grateful to my old friend Paul Andreu for his paintings that make my poetry book so beautiful. I also wish to extend my gratitude to the masters Luo Hanchao and Zhao Lihong. They spent precious time reading my poems and writing the preface to my book. I was extremely moved. Special thanks also go to my old friends Chen Xin and Wang Weisong. Without their sincere support and the efforts made by Shanghai People's Publishing House, this poetry book would not be published as scheduled.

Last but not least, I wish to thank you all once again, my dear readers, masters and friends, for the passion and inspiration you have offered to me, making my heart as young and pure as ever.

Written at Longingfield, Vermont, the United States
On the 15th of the seventh lunar month in 2016

Paul Andreu's painting No. 13